WAR OF WORDS

To Dallas and Nancy. While we may disagree about how to get there, I know we both have the same goal in mind. "For where your treasure is, there will your heart be also" (Matthew 6:21). Thank you for your constant friendship and support.

WAR OF WORDS

JEFFREY ARCHER NESBIT

VICTOR BOOKS

A DIVISION OF SCRIPTURE PRESS PUBLICATIONS INC.
USA CANADA ENGLAND

THE CAPITAL CREW SERIES
Crosscourt Winner
The Lost Canoe
The Reluctant Runaway
Struggle with Silence
A War of Words
The Puzzled Prodigy

Cover illustration by Kathy Kulin-Sandel

Library of Congress Cataloging-in-Publication Data

Nesbit, Jeffrey Asher.
   A war of words / Jeffrey Asher Nesbit.
     p. cm. — (The Capital Crew series: #5) (A Winner Book)
   Summary: When Cally and some classmates try to start a Bible
club at school, they have trouble with the principal and their dispute
escalates when the media and lawyers get involved.
   ISBN 0-89693-076-9
   [1. Freedom of religion — Fiction. 2. Schools — Fiction.
3. Christian life — Fiction. 4. Clubs — Fiction.] I. Title. II. Series:
Nesbit, Jeffrey Asher. Captial crew: 5. III. Series: Winner book.
PZ7.N4378War   1992
[Fic] — dc20   92-27663
                                                    CIP
                                                    AC

---

1 2 3 4 5 6 7 8 9 10 Printing/Year 96 95 94 93 92

VICTOR BOOKS
A division of SP Publications, Inc.
Wheaton, Illinois 60187

1

I should have known it was trouble. But I didn't, of course. I never see trouble until it's right in front of me.

It was such a simple idea. A bunch of kids sitting around in a classroom, talking about the Bible. Harmless, right?

I mean, all these other kinds of clubs meet after school. One more wouldn't cause much of a stir.

It was Elaine's idea. So what else is new? I think she spends half her day just dreaming up things like this.

She sort of banged into me between classes at Roosevelt one day and reminded me that I'd already said yes to her crazy idea and that we'd even talked to the principal about it a little.

I didn't remind *her* right away that the principal, John Kamber, hadn't seemed too keen on the idea then.

"Remember the Bible Club? Well, it's all set. We're ready to go," she told me breathlessly. "Isn't that great?"

"What?" I asked.

"You know," she frowned. "A Bible club, like the Chess Club or the Book Club. Something like that."

"I *know* what a Bible club is," I said grumpily. "What I mean is, what's this about it being all set?

Kamber hasn't said we could go ahead yet, has he?"

"I figured we could just let him know we were start-ing one," Elaine said with that dead-straight-ahead look of hers.

I sighed. When Elaine got that look, there was no stopping her.

"You sure about this?" I asked anyway.

"Sure," she said confidently. "We'll announce it on bulletin boards, put an ad in the school newspaper. Word of mouth too. It'll get around."

I thought for a second. "Shouldn't we at least make sure Kamber says it's OK?"

Elaine shook her head emphatically. "I've already got a teacher who's told me we can use her classroom after school. That's all we need . . ."

I persisted. "But shouldn't we make sure that Kamber . . ."

"Cally, come on! You heard him. If we wait for his answer, he might say no. Let's just start the club, then he can't stop it."

Somehow, somewhere, a little bell or alarm should have gone off in my head. But it didn't. Like I said, I never see trouble coming at me until it's too late to get out of the way.

"I don't know," I said slowly.

"Are you in or not?" Elaine Cimons asked crisply.

"All right, I'm in," I grumbled. "But I still think we ought to clear it with the principal."

"We'll do that later, if we have to."

"So how many members do you have signed up so far?"

Elaine smiled. "Just two, you and me. But don't worry. There'll be more. Lots more."

Why in the world our mother wanted to join the PTA is beyond me. The world famous PTA, the Parent-Teachers Association, is about the biggest snooze in history, if you ask me.

These parents sit around for *hours* and argue about all sorts of silly stuff. Like whether to put locks on the restroom stalls to keep kids from smoking in them. Or whether to post sentries outside the lunchroom to keep kids from kissing.

I could have saved them all a lot of grief and time. Just ban school and kids. Then you wouldn't have any smoking or kissing on school grounds.

"But *Mom!*" I pleaded with her. "Why do you wanna go listen to a bunch of whiny parents at the PTA?"

"Because," she answered, with only the barest hint of a smile.

"Give me one good reason," I demanded.

"I don't have to."

"Yes, you do," I insisted.

"No, I don't."

"Come on! Why not?"

"Because I'm your mother, that's why," she said, laughing.

"That's no reason," I scowled.

Mom stopped putting the dishes away in the kitchen. She turned and looked at me for a moment. "Okay, here's the reason. With Jana and Karen joining you at Roosevelt this year, I just decided to pay a little more attention to the school system you are attending. Make sense?"

I shrugged. "Sure, but can't you do that just as well by listening to us at dinnertime?"

"The way I see it, this is my duty as a parent."

"Your duty?"

"To get involved."

"But the PTA's such a waste of time. I mean, who cares about that stuff anyway?"

"I do," she said firmly. "And other parents do as well. Don't you *want* me to pay attention to what you and the other kids are doing?"

"Well, yeah, sure, but you don't have to go overboard."

"I'm not, Cally," Mom chuckled. "I promise, I'll be good at these meetings. I won't say much at all."

I guffawed. "That's a laugh. You like to jump in."

"I'll be good at these, you wait and see."

"No way, Mom. I know you. They'll get all worked up over something, and you'll wade right in."

Mom cocked her head. "Well, I'll at least give it the old college try, how about that?"

"Whatever you want, Mom," I sighed. "But I still think you're just wasting your time."

Elaine Cimons went right to work. Just two days after our first conversation, she already had the announcements up on just about every bulletin board at Roosevelt. And she said an ad would appear in the next newspaper as well.

"Now we need people," she told me between classes.

Elaine had cornered me coming out of my English Lit. class. She seemed to know my schedule better than I did. She was always bumping into me outside my classes. I had no room to escape. None at all.

"Can't you just wait and see who shows up?" I offered.

A look of mock horror crossed Elaine's face. "Oh, no! We can't do that. We have to have a core, a center, a small group of people who are committed to this project. Besides you and me, of course."

"You do? Why's that?"

I tried not to grimace. Elaine had thrown me wholeheartedly into this kettle, for better or worse, whether I wanted to be in the soup or not.

" 'Cause it shows the school we're serious about this, that we won't just go away."

I was slightly confused. "But why do we have to do *that*? Show the school we're serious about this?"

Elaine moved closer to me, almost touching me. She

glanced to her left and right, before whispering, "In case they try to stop us, that's why."

I shook my head. "Why would they try to stop us? And who are you talking about, anyway?"

"Oh, you know, the parents who wouldn't want to see a Bible Club at a public school, that's who," Elaine said. "People get all spooked when you start talking about Jesus and religion in public schools. It gets all mixed up in the stuff about separating church from things like schools, which are paid for by the government. There's supposed to be this separation of the church and the state. It's in the Constitution."

I turned to leave. "Ah, nobody'll care so much. It's harmless."

Elaine gave me a funny look, as if I'd just flown in from Mars or something. "You'll see. But can you do me a favor?"

"What is it?" I asked nervously, trying to edge away. Elaine's "favors" were always real doozies. Like standing outside some bookstore giving pamphlets away on a Saturday while everyone else was trying out the new skateboard park that had opened up around the corner. Somehow, Elaine was always a step, or three, off the beaten path.

"Can you talk to Barry and Jason?" she pleaded. "Make sure they're on board? I'll talk to Sheryl."

I groaned inwardly. She was talking about Barry Grimes, Jason Pittman, and Sheryl Thompson, the other members of our little Bible study that had tried—and failed—to get through the Book of James over the summer.

We'd fought over nearly every passage, over every nuance and interpretation. Sheryl was always reading something from the women's movement into the passages. Jason wanted everything done *exactly* the way the book said it had to be. And Barry was always chasing after some cloud or another.

It had been a hopeless task, trying to get through the study. Elaine gave it a heroic effort. She had pleaded, begged, and cajoled all summer long. To no avail. We came to a screeching halt about two thirds of the way through the book.

"But why them?" I asked her. "I mean, we never got through James. Why do you think they'd be interested now?"

"Oh, that study was different," Elaine scoffed. "For the Bible Club, we *need* fights and arguments. That's what will make it fun for everybody."

I almost laughed. "Yeah, well, Jason and Sheryl will fight, all right. About everything."

"Fights will be good, trust me," Elaine said. "Healthy. It'll make the club interesting."

"If you say so."

"So you'll talk to Barry and Jason?"

"Sure, no sweat," I said. "I'll talk to them for you."

"You won't regret it, Cally," Elaine said confidently. "This will be a great experience."

Yeah, sure, I thought. About as much fun as mowing the lawn each week or doing my math homework.

4

Barry Grimes was so excited he couldn't stop moving.

"Oh, cool, *cool!*" he said, running his hands through his short, brown hair. Actually, he wasn't running his hands through his hair, he was sort of rubbing his right hand back and forth through the stubble on top of his head, like you'd rub a rabbit's foot for luck.

As usual, Barry's clothes didn't come close to matching on the particular day I accosted him in the hall to sign him up for our Bible Club. His shirt was an ugly green plaid, while his pants were yellow, I think, and striped.

Once, during an especially awkward and tedious Bible study, I'd tried to count the freckles on Barry's face; I gave up when I got into the hundreds. Barry was definitely the freckle king.

"Yeah, it'll be great," I told him, trying to keep my lack of enthusiasm for this project from showing.

"But will they let us get away with this?"

"Who?"

"Ah, you know, like the principal."

"Do *you* think Kamber will care?"

"Yeah, sure," Barry shrugged. "You know he will. He always sticks his big, fat nose into stuff like this."

"Huh," I grunted. "You may be right. But Elaine says she's got all that covered. I think she already had a teacher who'll let us use her room after school."

"That doesn't mean ol' Kamber said OK to the deal though," Barry mused.

Good old John Kamber, our fearless principal. Stiff, proper, always neat and tidy as he wandered through the school's corridors, on the prowl for trouble.

I'd only had one other run-in with Kamber since I'd been at Roosevelt, just a few weeks after I'd arrived in Washington, D.C. My mom had just separated from my dad, who'd run off with some floozy in Birmingham, Alabama, after the steel mill where he'd worked his whole life had laid him off for good.

She moved the family of seven kids—I'm the oldest—up to Washington. We lived with my Uncle Teddy and Aunt Franny until Mom could afford to rent a place of her own.

My dad, by the way, had tried counseling for a while. He really had. He tried to quit all his boozing, and he started going to this counselor. But, like always, it didn't last long. He was back to his old ways again, drinking all the time and sort of drifting from one place to the next.

I'm the only one of the kids who knows this, but Uncle Teddy found Mom a lawyer recently, and I heard them talking about it late one night. Mom's going to file the divorce papers against Dad soon, which is just great as far as I'm concerned.

Dad is gone from our lives now, which is just as well. He's not a part of my life, that's for sure. I don't even think about him much anymore. Oh, I wish he was better and that he would change. But he won't change. I know that now.

It was shortly after we'd moved up to Washington, away from my dad, that I got into a stupid fight at school. Kamber took one look at the both of us and kicked us out of school for three days.

It had cost me my chance to play for Roosevelt's tennis team that year. I was horribly disappointed, and I was sure I would never recover.

But I did recover, of course. In fact, I more than recovered. That winter, perhaps driven over the stupidity of having been kicked out of school and off the tennis team, I beat my archenemy, Evan Grant, to win the national indoor tennis championships.

And this year, I was sure to make the Roosevelt tennis team. I had no doubt of that. And Evan Grant was now almost a friend and tennis partner. Almost.

"You're right," I told Barry. "Kamber's likely to be trouble. If he doesn't like this, there's no way it'll fly."

"Yeah, if he thinks it's a dumb idea, like maybe it's against the church and state separation thing, then it isn't going to happen."

"Well, I guess we'll see," I shrugged.

* * * * * * * *

Jason Pittman's reaction to my news was completely different from Barry's, which was to be expected. The two of them never agreed on anything. Never.

Jason didn't say anything right away when I told him about the Bible Club. He stood there in the hallway for about a hundred seconds in total silence. He adjusted and readjusted his wire rim glasses. He hitched his nicely creased pants once and fingered the top button of his pressed shirt.

"Now, let's see," he said very thoughtfully when he finally spoke. "What needs to be done? What must we do to make this a reality?"

"I, um, think that Elaine's pretty much taken care of everything," I offered.

Jason grimaced. "I doubt *that*. Elaine means well. But she sometimes skips right past the details. Life is won or lost in the details, you know."

I *know!* I almost screamed at Jason. I'd heard that kind of phrase, about life being won or lost in the details, a thousand times from Jason if I'd heard it once.

"Well, Elaine thinks she's done what needs to be—"

"Has she filed her charter with the school's staff secretary?" he interrupted me.

I didn't even know the school had a staff secretary. And I didn't have a clue what a charter was. But I wasn't about to let on to Jason. No way.

"Jason, I think she's done those kinds of things," I answered. "She seems to think Kamber and the principal's office isn't going to be a problem."

But Jason wasn't even paying attention to me. I could see that the "details" of our little project were, even now, beginning to swirl madly around in his head. By the end of the day, Jason would have a battle plan, a strategic map of action.

"Yes, yes, I'm sure," he mumbled. "But just in case, I'd better talk to Elaine about this. If we're going to make this work, then we'd better get moving."

You know, I have to say that I, for one, am very, very glad that there are Jason Pittmans in the world. For, without them, almost nothing would ever be accomplished. Because, as much as it pains me to admit this, life really *is* won or lost in the details.

"Great, Jason," I said, working up a smile. "You do that. Go find Elaine. Get it all worked out."

"I will, I will," Jason said, a starry-eyed look still plastered all over his face. "And thanks, Cally. Thanks for letting me know."

So, there it was. We had a Bible Club. None of us knew then what we were getting into. But, of course, we never really know that about a lot of things, do we? We go through life hoping the next moment doesn't swallow us up like the whale did Jonah.

Our first meeting was set for Wednesday after school, the last week of September. Elaine figured that if we held it in the middle of the week, we'd get more kids to at least drop by.

Kids will forget to come by on Monday because their brains aren't turned on yet. On Tuesday, they're desperately trying to figure out how they're going to get all their schoolwork done. Thursday's out because they're already starting to think about the weekend. And Friday's, well, a Friday. So Wednesday was the day.

Elaine was frantic beyond belief on Monday and Tuesday. She was matched only by Jason, who went around with a constant look of torment and pain etched deeply into his face.

The charter was on file in the principal's office. We had permission from a teacher to use her room after school. The ad had been placed in the school newspaper, and the flyers had mostly survived on bulletin boards around the school. Only a few had suffered at the hands of frustrated artists.

The school had buzzed, a little, over the event. Roosevelt had never had a Bible Club, at least not that anyone could remember, and it was kind of a novelty. Not that this meant anyone would actually show up.

When the Great Day arrived, I thought about skipping Bible Club. But then I also thought about how Elaine would absolutely kill me. There was no choice. I had to go.

The school day ended at 3 o'clock, and the clubs usually started 15 minutes after that. Naturally, I hung around my locker until 3:14 before I meandered over to Room 122, which was on the ground floor of the building, along the street that ran in front of Roosevelt.

Elaine and Jason were standing outside the classroom, greeting kids as they came in. Jason looked especially solemn. Elaine just looked worried.

"About time you got here," Elaine half-whispered. "We were wondering if you were going to show up."

"I, um, had something I had to take care of," I answered.

"Well, you could have gotten here a *little* earlier," Jason said.

I figured I'd better shift gears. "So how's the turnout?" I asked brightly.

Elaine beamed. "It's great! More than a dozen kids have shown up. That's more than I'd hoped for. It's a great nucleus."

I glanced at Jason. The scowl on his face was the worst I'd ever seen on him, which is saying something. "What's wrong, Jase?" I asked.

Jason glanced over his shoulder nervously. "You'll see when you go in there. There aren't just kids in the room."

"Whatcha mean?" I asked, straining to take a peek around the corner.

"There are teachers in there too," Elaine said. "And a couple of parents."

"Teachers? And parents?" I said, my eyes wide. "You've gotta be kidding!"

"No, we're not," Jason scowled. "There are four teachers in there right now. They just keep wandering in."

This time I moved around the corner and stared in. Off in the back of the room, sitting together in the corner, I counted six adults. Something about it really struck me funny. I almost started laughing.

"That's a switch," I grinned at Elaine.

"What is?"

"Usually, it's the kids who try to hide at the back of the room," I said. "Now it's the other way around, with the teachers at the back of the room and the kids sitting up front."

Elaine smiled too. "That's funny. You're right. I never thought about it that way."

"Well, *I* don't think there's anything funny about it," Jason said ominously. "I think it means trouble. Why are they here? Why would they come to something like this?"

Elaine glanced at me and shrugged. "Well, we'll know in a little bit. We should get started, I guess."

Jason and I nodded in agreement, then we all trooped into the room. Instinctively, none of us really looked at the adults in the back of the room. We all just sort of pretended they weren't there.

I counted fourteen kids sprawled in the desks toward the front of the room. I didn't recognize any of them, other than Sheryl Thompson, who had been the fifth member of our Bible study at Elaine's house this past summer, and Barry Grimes. The rest were strangers to me.

While Elaine sat down on the teacher's desk, Jason and I took two seats in the front row.

"I'm glad you all came today," Elaine said, her voice showing no fear at all. It was strong and clear. I marveled again at her courage. She never seemed to doubt what she was doing, not for a minute.

As Elaine was talking, I looked around at the various kids who'd shown up. Most of them were a lot like Barry. They all looked like they'd gotten dressed in the dark.

And then my eyes settled on this one girl, kind of sitting off to the side by herself. I'd seen her around school before. I think maybe she was a cheerleader. I vaguely remembered seeing her cheering at our first football game.

She had long, reddish-blond hair. More red than blond. She was wearing a soft, pink-and-white sweater. And she was absolutely beautiful. I found myself suddenly short of breath.

The girl looked over at me. Our eyes locked. She smiled shyly. I smiled back and then, because I could feel my face turning red, looked away. I had lost all track of time and reality. Elaine's words were a blur. The room was spinning a little.

" . . . so maybe we can go around the room first?" Elaine was saying. "Say your name, and then maybe say what you'd like to accomplish here in our Bible Club. Jason, why don't you go first?"

I looked over at Jason and breathed a big sigh of relief. If Elaine had turned to me first, I'd have been a dead duck. I probably would have gotten *my* name wrong.

Jason, predictably, began by talking about Ecclesiastes and what that particular book of the Bible meant to us today. Jason loved that book for some reason.

Maybe because it was so gloomy and foreboding.

I sank back in my seat and looked toward the front of the class. Elaine was staring at me, hard. There was murder in her eyes. I looked back at her. She glanced over at the girl with the reddish-blond hair and then back at me. Then she turned her attention to Jason.

"Thanks, Jason," Elaine said when he'd finished. "Now, let's go around the room."

I didn't listen too closely as the rest of the kids said their names. I was terrible with names anyway. The only one I paid any attention to was the mystery girl.

"Hi! My name's Lisa Collins," she said when it was her turn. "And I'll study whatever the group wants. Whatever you guys like is just fine with me." And then she smiled. My heart pounded.

When the last kid had finished, Elaine leaned forward. "Okay, great. Now, I thought before we got started, that maybe we'd all bow our heads and say a prayer, just to thank God for the meeting today and to give us strength and guidance—"

"You can't do that, young lady!" a loud voice said from the corner of the room.

All our heads jerked around as one. We all stared toward the six adults in the back corner of the room.

"Can't do what?" Elaine asked quietly.

"Say a prayer. Not in *this* classroom, you can't," answered a woman with a nose that was long and pointed and hair that was steel gray and pulled back tight. She sort of reminded me of a bird. A hawk, maybe.

"Why not?" Elaine asked the knot of adults.

"Because the Constitution forbids prayer in the public schools," said a second adult, a middle-aged man with a thick head of brown hair. He was wearing a nice tweed jacket and pressed blue jeans.

"You *do* know what the Constitution is, don't you, young lady?" a third adult added sarcastically. The other adults nodded.

"Well, um, yes, of course I know what the Constitution is," Elaine said feebly. "But I don't think it says anything about saying a prayer in our club here at Roosevelt—"

"Oh, it most certainly does speak to that," the hawk lady said angrily. "It most certainly *does!* There will be no state religion. There is a clear line between church and state."

I couldn't sit still any longer. Elaine needed some help. "But it's just a prayer," I said. "Not a state religion. It's just a prayer."

"You can't have the government promoting religion, not in the public schools," answered the hawk lady. "The Supreme Court does not allow this kind of thing on school grounds."

"But the state isn't sponsoring this, I am," Elaine said, confused. "I don't see the state around here anywhere."

"If prayers are uttered here," the hawk lady said, half rising from her seat, "then the state—the government—has a hand in it. The state becomes part of this vileness."

"No, it doesn't," I insisted. "It's just us. Nobody else."

"I have a question for you, young lady," began a fourth adult. "Have you obtained permission to hold this club on school grounds? Have you?"

"Well, yes, the teacher said we could use this classroom . . ."

"No, I mean permission from the administrator of this school," the adult said.

"We've filed a charter with the staff secretary of the school if that's what you mean," Jason said, deciding to join the fray.

"Not the same thing," said the hawk lady. "Do you have written permission from John Kamber, our principal?"

I glanced at Elaine. "No, not written permission," Elaine said. "But we let him know we are having this club."

The adults all glanced at each other. A few of them began to smile and several rose to their feet.

"Well, then, I think this little club is over for today," the hawk lady said gleefully. "I strongly suggest that you wait until you have permission from Mr. Kamber before you try to start it up again." The rest of the adults began to nod in agreement.

"But, we just wanted to say a prayer," Elaine said slowly, staring directly at the hawk lady.

"You get permission first, young lady," the man in the tweed jacket said sternly. "If you get it, then you can say your prayer."

Elaine looked back at me. There was nothing to be done. We both knew it. The first meeting of the Roosevelt Bible Club was officially over. I wondered if there would ever be a second meeting.

6

"So *now* what do we do?" Barry wondered out loud after the meeting had disbanded.

Barry and Sheryl had stuck around after everyone else had left, joining Jason and Elaine and me. The five of us were sort of lounging around at the front of the class, feeling miserable, to say the least, at the sudden turn of events.

We all looked at each other. No one said anything. Each of us, I was sure, had the same sinking feeling, that there was nothing much to be done.

After all, these were adults. Four of them were teachers. They'd all go complain to Kamber and that would be that. After hearing their complaints, he'd never give us permission to hold the Bible Club on school grounds, not in a million years.

"We at least have to go talk to Kamber," Jason said dully.

"Yeah, let's go talk to him, see what he has to say," Sheryl added. "Maybe he won't say no, maybe he'll be reasonable about it."

"And maybe pigs'll fly, and the moon will turn to cheese too," Barry grimaced. "There's no way. The cards are stacked against us."

Elaine gave me a funny look. "You know, we could send in an ambassador, like that cheerleader, Lisa Collins. What do you think about that, Cally?"

I perked up. "Hey! That's not a bad idea. I mean, she could—"

"It was a *joke*," Elaine said, her face darkening into a scowl. "I wasn't serious."

"Oh," I said, confused.

"Let's all go, the five of us," Sheryl said. "We'll go by to see Kamber first thing tomorrow morning. With all of us there, maybe he won't say no as easily."

Jason nodded. "He'll probably turn us down right away and then kick us out of his office, but I think you're right, Sheryl. We have to try."

"Well, before we do, I have a question," Elaine said.

"What?" Jason and Sheryl asked at the same time.

"Did any of you have a clue what those people were talking about?" Elaine said.

"About the separation of church and state?" asked Jason.

"And what, exactly, that has to do with our little Bible Club," Elaine nodded. "It doesn't make a whole lot of sense."

Jason shrugged, as if this kind of a fight was old hat to him. "Oh, my folks say it's been this way for years. They say a bunch of federal judges decided that the public school system was the state and that any mention of a religion in school meant the state was approving it."

"Roosevelt is a state?" Elaine asked. "It's just a school."

"Yeah, but it's a school that's paid for by people. We don't pay any tuition to come here, so it's kind of supported by the state," Jason said.

"So that makes it a state?" I asked.

"In a roundabout way, I guess," Jason answered.

"And, because it's the state, you can't talk about religion here?" Elaine said.

"Not on the school grounds, you can't," Jason said. "At least, there are some people who would argue that. My folks think it's all a bunch of nonsense. They think you should be able to say prayers in school, or have Bible Clubs, or do anything you want like that."

"Why do they think that?" Barry asked.

"Because the way they see it," Jason explained, "the state isn't exactly pushing religion unless its leaders are out there talking about it and junk like that. Kids like us doing what we want to in school is something totally different."

"I see," Elaine said thoughtfully. "I think that makes sense. We don't represent the state. We aren't its leaders . . ."

"Not yet, at least," Barry said ruefully.

Elaine laughed. "Yeah, that's right. And until we are the leaders, we aren't, like, setting up a state religion or any of that nonsense those parents were talking about."

"What really bugs me," Barry continued, "is that they're telling us we can't talk about certain things in school. That seems crazy."

"Yeah, it does," Sheryl added. "They can't do that."

"I mean, this is a free country," Barry said, getting worked up. "I thought we were supposed to be able to say whatever we wanted."

"That's the way it's *supposed* to be," Sheryl agreed.

"Well, this isn't anything like that," Barry said. "They're trying to make us be quiet. It's just not right."

"So let's go tell ol' Kamber just that!" Sheryl said excitedly.

I glanced at my watch. I had to leave to go to tennis practice. "You guys go without me if you're planning to go now. I have tennis practice."

"Can't you skip it just once?" Sheryl asked.

I scowled back at her. "C'mon, Sheryl, you can't do stuff like that. If you're in school, you have to go to practice."

"But nobody will notice," Sheryl persisted. "Come on with us. We need you."

I shook my head and began to edge out of my seat. "Nope, sorry. I have to go to practice."

Elaine held up a hand before Sheryl could continue. "We can't get in to see Kamber right now anyway. It's too late. So what I'll do is tell the secretaries that we need to see him first thing in the morning before school starts. Can everyone be here a half hour early tomorrow?"

I groaned. It was hard enough just getting to school on time, much less a half hour early. "I'll have to get my mom to drive me here, but I can make it."

"How about everybody else?" Elaine asked. "Can you make it?" Everyone else nodded slowly. "Great! Then we'll meet in Kamber's office tomorrow morning and give it our best shot."

"And if we fail?" Jason asked.

Elaine suddenly began to smile from ear to ear. It was almost a devious smile. She'd been thinking about this. I could see it. She had a plan, a good one. "Oh, we'll see. Let's wait and see what happens tomorrow. This isn't over yet. No way."

Tennis tryouts had started two weeks earlier.
This year was a *lot* different than last year. Because
both Evan and I had both done so well in tournaments
last winter and then over the summer, we were both
on the team almost automatically.

Everybody was picking us to win the Virginia State
Tournament. I mean, it made sense. Evan and I would
probably win all our singles matches during the
course of the year, no matter which one of us was
number one.

But there were five other matches in each competition
—two more singles and three doubles. And we weren't
certain of always winning those, not by a long shot.

The way Coach Kilmer had it figured, he'd split
Evan and me up, making two doubles teams that
should win their matches. It looked good on paper.
The only problem was that it didn't really quite work
that way.

Neither of the two kids who were likely to be third
and fourth on the team this year were great by any
means. They could play okay, but there was no guarantee that either Evan or I could always win a doubles
match with them as our partners.

Actually, an idea had been percolating in the back
of my mind for some time. I was just waiting to spring
it on Coach Kilmer.

You see, Evan Grant and I had actually been playing some doubles together. He and I would join as a team at the club and play some of the adults. We never lost, not even when Steve Walker, the club pro, hooked up with someone.

Evan and I were deadly together. There was no way around it. With my serve and backhand, and his consistent ground strokes, we played very well together. Maybe even good enough to win the nationals this year against the older fourteen-year-olds.

Plus, there were these two ninth-graders who'd been on Roosevelt's team for the past two years. They weren't very good at singles, but they were a great doubles team, when they played third. They almost never lost.

So if Evan and I played first-team doubles, and the ninth-graders played third, we could do it. I was sure of it. Of course, I hadn't sprung this on Evan yet. I wasn't sure how he'd react.

I forgot about the Bible Club as soon as I was outside and heard the "plunk, plunk" of tennis balls whizzing back and forth over the net. My mind shifted gears instantly. School was over, and I was free. At least, for a couple of hours.

"Let's hit a few, Deep South," Evan joked when I arrived at courtside.

I gave him a dirty look. He hadn't ribbed me with that nickname for some time, not since we'd stopped being archenemies. "You think you can keep up with me?" I asked him.

"You've got it backward," Evan said. "You'll have to worry about keeping up with me."

"In your dreams," I laughed.

My cares melted into oblivion as soon as the first ball was in play. There was nothing else in the world I cared about at that particular moment. My entire mind and body were focused on just one thing—following the flight of the fuzzy, yellow ball and returning it to the other side with as much force as I could muster.

"Hey, slow down!" Evan yelled at me from the other side of the net after a few minutes. "You'll wear yourself out before practice starts."

I took a deep breath. Evan was right. I was so wound up from the confrontation at the Bible Club that I'd been crushing the ball. I waved my racket at Evan.

Evan suddenly zinged one crosscourt, almost out of reach. I took two quick steps across the court and flicked my racket at it. The ball floated lazily over the net, landing about three quarters of the way into Evan's side.

Evan took the ball on the short hop and sent a forehand screaming down the line to my backhand side. Then he rushed the net. He was attacking fiercely, just when my guard was down.

I lunged at the ball and lofted a high lob over Evan's head. Evan scrambled back and tried to hit an overhead for a winner. I was able to get my racket on it and arch another lob in the air. Evan tried another smash, but it wasn't deep enough, and I was able to hit a pretty decent forehand back at him.

Evan took the volley and tried to angle it away from me. I saw the shot coming though, and sprinted toward it. I got to the ball before it could bounce a second time and flicked it away from Evan, across his backhand.

He just barely got a racket on it and put up a defensive lob of his own. I raced back for the ball. I didn't even hesitate. I leaped up high and took the ball in the air. I creamed the overhead for a winner.

Evan dropped his racket to the ground in mock anger. "One of these days," he muttered, "I'm gonna learn how to play the net."

I grinned broadly. "You think so, huh?"

"Yeah, I think so," Evan said. He approached the net, leaving his racket on the ground. "So what's eatin' at you anyway?"

I joined him at the net and recounted the story of our Bible Club. I told him how bleak the picture looked now. Evan just nodded thoughtfully as I told him the story.

"You know, you'll need a good lawyer," he said when I'd finished.

"A lawyer? What for?"

Evan gave me a strange look. "You don't really think you're going to get Kamber to agree to this, do you?"

I frowned. "Well, no, I guess not."

"Then you'll need a lawyer. He'll have to represent you when you challenge the school."

"Why would we do that?"

Evan sighed. "Boy, sometimes, Cally, I wonder about you. How else are you going to get them to let you hold your dumb little club?"

"It isn't dumb," I said testily.

"Oh, you know what I mean," Evan said soothingly.

"You oughtta come to it, you know," I challenged him. "It would be good for you."

"You win against the school," Evan said, "and I'll come to one of your meetings. But you won't win, not without a good lawyer."

"And you can find one of those?"

Evan nodded forcefully. "I sure can. Just leave it all up to me."

It was going to be one of those days. I slept through the alarm. It never even made a dent in my consciousness. Then I absolutely, positively could not find two socks that matched each other. I finally had to settle for one navy blue and one black.

Mom didn't say much as she drove me to school early. I could see that she was dead tired these days. There were plenty of demands on her at work, which she didn't talk about much. I knew she liked what she was doing though.

The reason Mom was so tired was that she'd begun taking a couple of courses at night at George Mason University, just down the road. Aunt Franny came over on those nights.

Mom really hadn't said too much about her decision to go back to school. All she'd said was that she'd written a letter to some folks at the university, gone by to see them, and they'd told her that she could earn her degree if she took some courses in the fall, the spring, and then the summer.

And then, I knew what she meant to do. I was pretty sure she meant to take the Foreign Service exam. And what happened after that was anybody's guess. I tried not to think about it too much.

All I knew was that I trusted Mom. Completely. If she said to move a mountain, I'd do my best to move that mountain. If she said, pack up and move to Tibet, well, I'd be on the next plane out.

As far as I'm concerned, there's really no one else like my mom. Not in this world, at least. She took all the grief my crummy father handed out for all those years. And then, when the bum just up and ran off with someone else, my mom didn't complain. She just got on with her life and made a new home for her family.

My mom made it very easy to honor at least half of one of the Ten Commandments, the part about honoring your mother and father. I had a real tough time with that second part.

"You still haven't really told me what all this is about, you know, Cally," Mom said when we were sitting at a stoplight about halfway to school.

"Ah, it's this Bible Club thing Elaine got me into," I grimaced.

"Why? What's the problem?"

"Well, you know, we had our first meeting yesterday, after school. It was tame. We just kind of introduced ourselves and junk like that. But when Elaine tried to say a prayer, one of the teachers who was there stopped her."

"*One* of the teachers?" Mom asked. "How many were there?"

"I think there were four teachers, sitting in the back. And a couple of parents too."

Mom gripped the steering wheel harder. "You mean there were six adults at your first meeting?"

"Yep. Pretty weird, isn't it?"

Mom sighed. "No, not weird at all. Typical, if you ask me. You'd think it was a crime to be a Christian."

"Why do you say that?"

"Oh, people seem to get crazy when you start talking about religion in the public schools."

"But why, Mom? We talk about all sorts of weird junk in school, like sex and drugs and rock lyrics. Why can't we talk about the Bible? That seems harmless."

Mom smiled. "Actually, the Bible threatens some of those adults in your school more than anything else on earth. That's one of the reasons they fight so desperately to keep it out of your school."

I didn't say anything. The light turned green, and we drove for a few more blocks in silence.

"You know," she continued at the next red light, "I think I may have to bring this up at our next PTA meeting. It would set the place on its ear, but we may have no choice."

"I don't know, Mom; we're meeting with Kamber, the principal, this morning. Maybe you should wait and see how we do."

Mom glanced over at me. "I'll wait, Cally. Don't you worry about that. But I just don't think you'll be successful. If I know those teachers who showed up at your club yesterday, they've already been to see Kamber. I doubt very much if your arguments will persuade him of anything."

"We have to try though, don't we?"

"Sure, by all means. Give it your best shot. But if you don't succeed, I think I may want to do something about it. I hate taking things like this sitting down."

I tried not to give my mom a funny look. Boy, in the past year, she'd really become a fighter. No more nice guy. Or nice lady. She was taking on the world.

"You sure you want to get into this fight?" I asked.

"I'm sure," Mom nodded. "If it's all right with you."

I shrugged. "No skin off my nose. Just don't make too many parents mad."

"I'll try not to," Mom laughed. "But I can't promise that. We'll just have to see how it goes."

9

I was the last to arrive in Kamber's office. Elaine, Jason, Sheryl, and Barry were already there, sitting quietly in the chairs that ringed his outer office.

Jason, not surprisingly, had come well-armed for our little discussion. He had a couple of big, thick books with him, and I could see that he had a few places marked.

"What are those?" I asked him.

"Oh, just a few case histories," Jason answered.

"Case histories? Of what?"

"Of some Supreme Court decisions, and a couple of federal appeals cases as well," he said nonchalantly, as if he combed through that kind of thing all the time.

"Where in the world did you find them?" I asked, trying not to sound like an incredulous dope.

"Ah, you know, I've got an older brother in law school. He helped me look up the cases."

"Hmmm, I see," I said. "And you think they'll help?"

"They can't hurt." Jason grinned. "They're all about cases that involved religion in public. Like whether some guy could wear a yarmulke at work, stuff like that."

"So could he?" I asked.

"Could he what?" Jason said.

"Wear his yarmulke?"

"Sure," Jason nodded. "The judge said they had to let him wear it. Some of his coworkers said they were offended by it, but the judge said it was his individual right. You can't really stop someone, one person, from doing his own religious thing."

"Well, that's what we're doing, isn't it?" Sheryl chipped in. "Just expressing ourselves? Like that guy who wanted to wear his yarmulke?"

Jason pursed his lips. "I don't know. It's not really the same thing. That guy was just one person. The courts seem to get all spooked when you've got something organized, like teachers who want to say prayers in the classroom."

"So do you have anything in there that talks about Bible clubs in school?" Barry asked.

"No," Jason said. "We couldn't find anything on that. We tried, but it's apparently not something anyone's ever gone to court over."

"Maybe we'll be the first," Elaine laughed. "If ol' Kamber says no, I mean."

I leaned over so the secretaries couldn't hear me. I could see that they were trying to listen to our conversation without appearing as if they were. "You know," I whispered, "Evan Grant says he'll find us a good lawyer."

"Really? That's great," Elaine whispered back.

"Shouldn't we wait to see—" Sheryl started to say, but then stopped in mid-sentence as Kamber suddenly strode out of his office.

"Well, this is *certainly* unusual!" he boomed as he approached us. "Five students here early. That's one for the record books. Come on, come on, let's go into my office and talk about our little problem. Let's see if we can't work something out."

We all trooped into his office silently. Five chairs were neatly arranged in a semicircle around his desk. Kamber seemed to be well-prepared for our visit.

Elaine took the seat squarely facing Kamber. The rest of us eased into the remaining four chairs. Elaine leaned forward in her chair, eager for the discussion to begin.

"Miss Cimons, it's been awhile since you graced us with your presence," Kamber said as he settled into his nice brown chair, which creaked and groaned in complaint.

"Yes, sir, it has," Elaine answered.

"That's quite a cross hanging from your neck," Kamber observed, gazing up at the ceiling. "Rather big and obvious, wouldn't you say?"

"I'm proud of who I am and what I believe in," Elaine answered, instinctively reaching for the big, wooden cross that always hung from her neck. She turned it over in her hands a couple of times.

"Yes, I can see that," Kamber said.

"You're not going to say anything about *that,* I hope," Elaine said.

"Oh, heavens, no!" Kamber laughed good-naturedly. "I just noted it in passing, that's all. I've never seen anything quite like it."

Jason broke in quickly. "Mr. Kamber, have you had a chance to review our charter?"

Kamber turned his somber eyes on Jason. "Are you Mr. Pittman?" Jason nodded. "Well, son, yes, as a matter of fact, I have had a chance to review it."

"And it's in order, right?" Jason said, trying to lead him along.

"Well, let us get to that point in just a moment," Kamber said slowly. "First, I'd like to talk to the five of you about goals and objectives for a moment."

"Goals and objectives?" I asked.

"Yes, the goals and objectives of Roosevelt, what this place is all about, what we hope to accomplish,"

Kamber said, looking over my head, at the wall behind me.

"That's easy," Sheryl chimed in. "We're here to learn."

"Yes, yes, that's precisely right," Kamber nodded. "We are here to learn. Math, science, the arts, social studies, all of that. But there's more to it than that."

"There is?" Elaine asked.

"Why certainly," Kamber said soothingly. "We're also here to learn how to coexist as a community, how to live with shared values. For if we cannot learn that, then society will collapse in on itself."

"I don't understand," I said.

Kamber frowned. "Well, it's simple, really. If too many elements of society are at odds with each other, are warring against each other, then chaos reins supreme and society eventually disintegrates."

"What does all of that have to do with learning stuff at Roosevelt?" asked the ever-practical Jason.

"Well, son, it has a lot to do with learning at Roosevelt," Kamber said. "If there is discord and disharmony here at school, then the learning environment is disrupted. Children don't learn."

Elaine's eyes were as scrunched-up as I'd ever seen them. "Mr. Kamber, isn't democracy sort of about all kinds of different people and groups expressing themselves? Don't they have that right?"

Kamber swiveled slightly in his chair and gazed directly at Elaine. "Yes, that's what democracy is supposed to be about. But, in order for it to work properly, everyone must have a common goal, a similar objective. We must all be striving for the same thing."

Elaine leaned forward in her seat. "Mr. Kamber, what does all of this have to do with our Bible Club? I don't understand."

Kamber sighed. "I was trying to put this discussion in context for you. I want you to understand that Roosevelt is a community. For it to work, we must have shared values and beliefs. If any one group threatens that, then the place becomes a battleground and kids don't learn."

"Are you saying that our Bible Club is a threat to people?" Jason asked.

Kamber didn't say anything right away. When he did, his voice was cold and distant. "It is a force for disruption and chaos, yes. It cuts against the grain of what kids in this school are all about. I would wager that very few kids are walking on the same path as the five of you."

"But that's the whole purpose of our Bible Club, to teach kids about that," Elaine said.

Kamber's jaw tightened. "Not in this school, you won't. You cannot preach Christianity here. It simply will not be tolerated."

I could see that Elaine had made a mistake by talking about telling kids about Christ through the Bible Club. I decided to change directions quickly. "Mr. Kamber, our club is for kids who believe in the same thing. We just want to meet and talk about it, that's all. Like kids who all like to play chess meet to do that."

Kamber glanced at me. "All well and good, I suppose. The problem is that other children and parents are disturbed by your actions. They don't share your values and beliefs."

"What?" Elaine almost screeched.

"One of the things we try to teach the children at Roosevelt is that we all live in one great, big community," Kamber said. "In order for that community to work, we must all believe that we can change things for the better by helping each other. We cannot rely on some distant or nonexistent God to intervene on our behalf."

"That's what school's supposed to be about?" Barry asked.

"Most certainly," Kamber nodded. "It is a place where children learn how to live in the adult community they will eventually become a part of. And that community helps itself. It doesn't rely on some invisible God to help it out. You must help yourself and each other."

Elaine looked at me. I don't think either of us could believe we were hearing this. To me, it sounded like Kamber was condemning us for being Christians, for believing in God. I wondered if she saw it that way.

"Mr. Kamber, I don't think I agree with you," Elaine said. "I'm not sure I understand everything you've said. But it doesn't sound right to me."

"Young lady, you don't necessarily have to agree with it," Kamber answered. "You just have to live with it, because it is the way a community functions. There can be no discord and disruption here. It cannot be tolerated."

"But we aren't trying to—" I tried to say.

"Mr. James!" Kamber interrupted. "When you got in that fight last year, what happened? What did I do?"

"You kicked me out of school for three days," I said glumly.

"Exactly," Kamber nodded. "And the same principle is at work here. If someone does something deliberate to provoke a battle or a confrontation, if someone picks a fight, then it is my duty as an administrator to stop that action because it disrupts the entire school."

"And you think our Bible Club does that?" Elaine asked.

Kamber nodded. "It most certainly does. Never before have so many teachers and parents complained about something."

"But why?" I asked innocently.

"The parents don't want their kids influenced by you," Kamber said. "And the teachers think you're disrupting things here. It makes it harder for them to teach about shared values."

We all sat there in stunned shock. This had not gone as any of us had imagined it would. We thought we were talking about a simple club, and Kamber had accused us of treason at the school.

"I guess this means you won't allow our club on the school's grounds?" Elaine said, her voice a bit wobbly.

Kamber looked up at the ceiling again for a moment. "I would hope," he said slowly, "that you would disband voluntarily. For your sake, for the school's sake. That would be the decent and honorable thing to do."

"You're not telling us we *can't* meet after school?" Elaine pressed.

"I'm asking you to reconsider what you've set in motion and to go about your real business at school. If you want to meet, then do it in your homes, or off the school grounds," Kamber said.

"And if we try to meet here at Roosevelt?" Elaine asked.

Kamber shook his head. "Please. Don't force my hand, Miss Cimons. It isn't wise. I would not advise you to do that."

"But if we try, what will happen?" Elaine persisted.

"Then I will be forced to take action against you," he said stiffly. "Because you would be meeting illegally. I have not accepted your club's charter. It is still under consideration in my office. Until I do render a decision on it, your club cannot and should not meet."

"But when *will* you rule on it?" I asked.

"I would hope that won't be necessary," Kamber said. "If the five of you dissolve the club right now, then there will be no hard feelings on any side and life will go on peaceably."

Elaine looked at the rest of us, just to see. She saw that none of us were wavering. "Mr. Kamber, I don't think we want to give anything up. We want to have our club. If you won't agree to our charter, then please tell us."

Kamber rose from his chair and extended a hand to Elaine. "Why don't you take some time to think about my offer? Talk it over with your parents. Once you've had a chance to think about things—to understand the *consequences* of your actions if you do the wrong thing—then perhaps you'll reconsider."

"Mr. Kamber, I think we know—" Elaine began.

"Just think about it," Kamber said, moving away from his desk toward the doorway. "That's all I ask. It is an important decision. For all of us."

10

We all dispersed after the session with Kamber without saying much to each other. There wasn't much to say anyway. While much of what Kamber had told us was hard to follow—at least for *me*—I knew what the bottom line was.

Kamber didn't want our Bible Club meeting at his school because teachers and parents would be upset. They'd complain to the school board, most likely, and the school board could make life difficult for good ol' Kamber and Roosevelt.

But what could we do now? I could feel my blood starting to boil. This was a fight we were in now. Not a physical fight, for sure, but a fight nevertheless. And I hate to lose fights, on the tennis court or anywhere else.

I think I knew what Elaine would want to do. She'd want to try to meet again, just to see what Kamber would do. Would he try to stop us? Would he send the police to keep us away?

Elaine grabbed me after our second class that day. I could see that she'd been thinking furiously too.

"I saw Kamber talking to Mrs. Sanders," Elaine said breathlessly, after she'd pulled me off to one side of the crowded hallway.

"Who?"

Elaine frowned. I thought she was going to hit me.

"You know, the teacher who let us use her classroom for the Bible Club."

"Oh, *that* Mrs. Sanders," I mumbled. "What do you think they were talking about?"

"I'm sure Kamber was telling her that she shouldn't let us use her room anymore."

"You think so?"

"Of course," Elaine said. "He's trying to head us off, without actually telling us we can't meet."

I shook my head. "Why's he doing that, do you think? Why doesn't he just tell us no?"

Elaine pursed her lips. "I think he's worried."

"Worried?"

"Yeah, about what might happen, if he told us no. If the word got around, I mean. If we all just go away quietly, then he's a hero to the parents and teachers who don't want us to meet, and the parents who might like to see a Bible Club at Roosevelt won't even know what happened."

"Do you really think there are people who would care whether our club met or not?"

"Sure. My folks would care. Your mom would care, I bet."

I thought about it for a moment. Yeah, Mom probably would care. In fact, she might even do something about it. She'd probably try to make trouble for Kamber if she could figure out how to do that.

"You may be right," I mused.

"I *know* I'm right," Elaine said.

I glanced at the clock. We had about a minute to get to our next class. "I gotta go," I said.

"Look, Cally. Meet me here after your next class," Elaine whispered fiercely. "We have to go talk to Mrs. Sanders."

"Why?"

Elaine put her hands on her hips. "Sometimes I could just strangle you, Cally. We have to go talk to her. If Kamber's convinced her not to let us in her classroom, then we're sunk."

"We can always find another classroom," I said, shrugging.

"No, we can't. I tried before. She was the only one I could find who would let us."

I was absolutely shocked. "You mean, she was the only teacher who would let us use her classroom after school?"

"For a Bible Club, yes. None of the other teachers wanted their room used for that. They wouldn't exactly tell me that, but they all said no when I asked."

The bell rang. We both jumped a little. "Elaine, that's kind of spooky, if you ask me."

"Yeah, I know. I thought it was too. But that's why we have to go talk to Mrs. Sanders. She's our only hope."

"Okay," I nodded. "I'll see you after the next class."

11

Mrs. Sanders was working at her desk when Elaine and I went to see her between classes. She was a very young woman, probably in her early twenties, and she still wore her hair long and sometimes wore jeans to school. All the kids liked her.

"Hi, Mrs. Sanders," Elaine said brightly.

"Elaine, how are you?" Mrs. Sanders said somberly.

"You know we had our first club meeting here the other afternoon," Elaine said.

"Mr. Kamber told me about it," Mrs. Sanders said, looking away. "He also said you wouldn't be meeting anymore, that you wouldn't be needing my classroom."

I could feel my blood starting to boil again.

"Mrs. Sanders," Elaine said quickly, "that isn't exactly true. We didn't tell Kamber that we weren't meeting anymore. We still want to if you'll let us use your classroom."

Mrs. Sanders looked down at some papers on her desk. "I just don't think I can."

"Why not? What did Kamber tell you?"

Mrs. Sanders looked up then. "Look, Elaine, I *need* this job. It's my very first one out of school, and if I fail at it, well, it will go with me the rest of my career. Kamber can really hurt me, if he wants to."

Elaine and I looked at each other. This was serious.

I don't think either one of us had quite expected this.

"Mrs. Sanders, we don't want to do anything that gets you in trouble," Elaine said. "Really, we don't. If you think Kamber will make trouble for you, then we'll have to try to find another classroom."

"Don't even bother, Elaine," Mrs. Sanders said softly. "He'll just go talk to that teacher as well. He won't threaten, but his message will be plain enough."

"So you think it's hopeless?" I asked.

"Cally? Is that your name?" Mrs. Sanders asked. I nodded. "Well, Cally, every teacher in this school answers to Kamber. Our performances are evaluated by him. If he wants to, he can end our careers."

I shuddered. "That's awful."

Elaine started to back away from the desk. "Look, we should be going. Thanks for trying, at least."

Mrs. Sanders closed her eyes for a second, almost as if she were praying. Then she opened them and stood up quickly. "Elaine, wait. Don't do anything just yet. Let me think about it, OK?"

"Sure, if you want," Elaine said.

"I just want to talk it over with my husband, see what he thinks. Don't give up on me just yet. I may surprise you."

"You don't have to worry about this," Elaine said. "Really. This isn't your fight. It's ours."

"No, Elaine, you're wrong," Mrs. Sanders said, her eyes blazing. "It's my fight too. It's all of ours. We're all part of it. Freedom of religion is a constitutional guarantee, and when someone interferes with that right, then it becomes everyone's concern."

"If you say so," Elaine said.

"I say so. Now go on. You'll be late for your next class."

Despite my better instincts, I let Evan drag us to a lawyer's office the day after good, ol Kamber had told us to go jump in the lake. Evan's dad took a little time off work and picked us up after tennis practice.

I have to admit, I sure felt strange going to a lawyer. In my mind, lawyers were trouble. Mom went to one to start getting a divorce from Dad. You went to lawyers when someone was giving you a hard time, or when someone was doing something crummy to you and you needed protection.

"So what, exactly, do we need a lawyer for?" I questioned Evan.

"To sue the school," Evan replied bluntly as we drove along.

"Oh, come on!" I laughed. "That's crazy."

"Why? What's so crazy about it?"

"Sue the school? Are you out of your mind? What would we sue them for? What do we want?"

"You want into that classroom, that's what you want."

"And we sue them to do that?"

Evan let out a big, theatrical sigh. "So tell me, how else are you planning to get into that classroom? Didn't Kamber say no?"

"Well, not exactly. He sort of did, but he also wanted us to decide for ourselves."

"Sure!" Evan exploded. "Of course he wouldn't come right out and say no to your face. He's a big coward. He wants this to just go away without anybody getting mad. He doesn't want a bunch of angry parents running around screaming at him."

"I can't blame him."

"Me either. But you still haven't answered my question. Is Kamber gonna let you in or not?"

"I guess not," I answered glumly.

"So, then, how else are you planning to get in without a lawyer?"

I thought about it for a second. "I was sort of hoping that we'd all just forget about this whole thing," I said finally.

Evan just stared at me like I'd lost my mind. "You aren't serious? You can't be."

"Why?"

He shook his head. "Are you a Christian or not? Do you believe in all that junk or not?"

"It isn't junk, Evan," I said testily.

"It must be junk if you'd just quit so easily when somebody tells you they don't want you talking about it in their school," Evan baited me.

"I'm not quitting."

"Sure you are," Evan said. "What else do you call it, if you're not willing to fight for what you believe in?"

"I'm willing to fight," I said, my face flushing a little with embarrassment. "I'm just not sure this is the right place to fight."

"You let yourself get rolled here, and you might as well just throw your Bible away if you ask me," Evan said evenly. "That's the way I see it."

I glanced toward the front of the car where Evan's dad had sat quietly throughout our conversation. "What do you think about all this, Mr. Grant?"

Evan's dad didn't look back. But our eyes met briefly in the rearview mirror. "Cally, I think Evan's exactly
right on this," he answered. "If this is something you
believe in, then you'd better fight for it. But it's your
choice. You'll have to decide."

I looked out the window at the passing trees. "You
know we can't afford to pay for a lawyer," I said
softly.

"Don't worry about that, Cally," Evan's dad said.
"I'll take care of that. The lawyer we're going to visit
has done a lot of work for me over the years. He's just
likely to take this case pro bono if I ask him to. And if
he doesn't, well, then I'll pay for it myself."

I looked toward the front of the car again. "Why
would you do that, Mr. Grant?"

"Because I believe in your fight, Cally, that's why,"
Evan's dad said with a smile. "I think you're right, and
I'd like to see you win the fight."

I looked back at Evan who was beaming from ear to
ear. "The two of you make a great team, you know
that," I told Evan.

* * * * * * * *

The lawyer was very persuasive. But, then I guess I
should have expected that. The guy was paid a lot of
money to be persuasive.

"Look, I see it this way," said the lawyer, Robert
Ritter, a pretty young guy who was starting to go bald
early. "We can file a class action lawsuit against the
school's principal, representing all those students
who are likely to be grieved by his decision."

"What?" I asked, not sure at all what he meant.

Rob smiled. "Sorry. A class action lawsuit means
you are representing a whole bunch of people who

might all care about what you're doing. In this case, it would be all the kids in school who might want to attend a Bible Club, if there was one."

"So what do you think the grounds would be, Rob?" Evan's dad asked.

Rob shrugged. "I'll have to think about it for a bit. This is brand-new, I'd guess. We'll have to come up with something novel, like maybe they've taken away one of their constitutional rights."

"Such as?" Mr. Grant pressed.

"Off the top of my head, I would say that the state has taken away their First Amendment rights," Rob said.

"What's the First Amendment about?" I asked.

"It's about free speech and freedom of religion in this country," Rob said. "The amendment guarantees both. It makes sure the government can't stop either. You're supposed to be able to say what you want, believe what you want."

"And you think, in this case, that's what the government has done?" Mr. Grant asked. "It has stopped freedom of religion?"

"Yes, I think a case can be made that Roosevelt, which is a public school and funded by the people, is an arm of the state. And it is clearly prohibiting the free exercise of religion."

"You mean, by keeping the kids from meeting, they're stopping freedom of religion?" Evan asked.

Rob nodded. "That's right. Most people think of the First Amendment as making sure the government doesn't set up a 'state religion.' That's what people are talking about when they say there's a line between church and state. But there's a second part, which people forget about. It's the part guaranteeing the government can't stop free expression of religion."

Mr. Grant clapped his hands together. "Rob, I think you have something here. That's what's happening. The school is keeping the kids from expressing their religious beliefs."

Rob smiled. "Of course, the argument from their side is that if the school lets the kids establish a Christian Bible Club on school grounds, then the state—that is, the government—is establishing a state religion."

"Oh, that's nonsense, and we all know it," Mr. Grant said. "They don't want the kids talking about the Bible at school, plain and simple. They're blocking their religious rights."

"Well, perhaps we'll see," Rob mused.

"Then you'll take on the case?" Mr. Grant asked.

"Yes, I will," Rob said without hesitation. "It's outside my area of expertise. I've never argued constitutional law before, but it'll be fun. I need a diversion."

"You'll take it pro bono?" Mr. Grant asked.

"Yes, sure, I'll do it gratis," Rob said. "I'll find the time."

I held up a hand. "There's one other thing you all should think about."

"What's that, Cally?" asked Rob.

"Well, Kamber, our principal, hasn't exactly said no to us yet. He told us he hoped we'd drop the whole thing on our own. But he hasn't actually said no."

Rob glanced at Mr. Grant. "So he hasn't completely closed the door on you yet?"

"Nope, not yet," I said.

"Then maybe we can settle this out of court," Rob said, drumming his fingers on the table as he thought. "I'll tell you what. Let's set up another meeting with him. And let me do the talking this time, OK?"

"Sure, OK," I said.

Rob looked down at a calendar on his desk. "This Friday okay for you two?"

I looked over at Evan. "He's not part of this," I said, jerking my head toward my friend. "Just me."

"No, no, I'm in this now," Evan said quickly.

"But you're not a . . ." I started to say.

"You never know about stuff like that, Cally," Evan said, looking me right in the eye. "But I'm in this now. I'm part of it."

"Sure, that's great," I said brightly, not sure what was going on in Evan's mind right now.

"So is Friday all right with you?" Rob asked. Evan and I both nodded in unison. "Great. Then it's set. I'll call the principal's office and set up a meeting, then I'll let you both know when it is so you can invite your other friends."

"And if it doesn't work?" I asked.

"Let's wait and see," Rob said. "But we have lots of options yet, up to and including a big, public fight, which I'm sure the school doesn't want."

13

It was funny, but every time I told somebody about what was happening, they got all excited. First Evan, then his dad's lawyer. Now my mom, who got about as hopping mad as I've ever seen anyone get.

"They can't *do* that!" she almost yelled that night over dinner.

"Sure they can," I said. "Kamber just did it."

"Why in the world would they keep you from reading the Bible in school?" Mom frowned. "It's the most ridiculous thing I've ever heard."

I glanced around the table at the rest of the kids. Timmy, who was a year and a half now, was separating his food as usual and dropping various parts of it on the floor or on the distant corners of his high chair.

The twins, Karen and Jana, were whispering fiercely to each other about some boy they'd both seen at school that day, a ninth-grader by the sound of it. Since Dad had finally dropped out of the picture for good, the two of them had grown as close as ever. Susan was listening in on Karen and Jana's conversation, totally fascinated.

John was diligently eating his dinner, bite by bite, as usual. He was also devouring a book as he ate, which was a little unusual for him. Mom almost never let the kids do anything like homework at the dinner table.

I glanced over to see what he was studying so diligently. It was a red book of some sort, filled with lots of big words, most of which I didn't know. He was spending more time on each page than usual, which really made me curious. I'd definitely have to ask John what he was up to.

Chris was gone, at a friend's house. He now had so many friends he could probably stay over for dinner at a different house every night for a month. I was sure Mom knew where he was tonight, but she was the only one who kept track of him. I'd given up.

Which left Mom and me. It might as well have been just the two of us having a nice conversation over dinner because the rest of the family sure wasn't paying any attention to us.

"Evan found us a lawyer," I said.

"Evan Grant? He's involved in this?"

I smiled. "Don't ask me why, but he is. He's even planning to come to the next Bible Club meeting, if we ever have one."

"But he's not a Christian, is he?"

"Beats me," I shrugged. "All he told me was that he was a part of the fight now and that you never know about stuff."

Mom shook her head. "Well, I'll be. I guess you don't know. Although, I do have to say, he's grown an awful lot in the past year or so. He was kind of a brat before, and now he's a pretty nice kid."

"Yeah, I know. I've been thinking I might ask him to play doubles with me for a couple of the winter tournaments. Maybe we could even go back to the indoor championships as a doubles team. We sure aren't gonna get too far in singles this year, with everybody a year older than us."

"Cally, that's a *wonderful* idea," Mom beamed. "The

two of you would make a great team."

"We'll see."

Mom's eyes got a little dreamy, like they always do when she's thinking about which way to go with something. "You know, there's something *I* can do about your Bible Club."

"What's that?"

"I can take the issue to the PTA, see what they think."

I coughed. "You think that's a good idea?"

"Why not?" Mom shrugged. "It can't hurt. If enough parents get riled, then it might force your principal to reconsider his position."

"But what if a whole bunch of parents get all upset about having a Bible Club in school?"

"Then we'll have a big fight on our hands, I guess," Mom laughed.

"Bigger than the one we already have?"

"Never underestimate the ability of parents to blow everything way out of proportion, Cally," Mom smiled. "They have a long history of doing that."

14

Somehow, the word had started to get around school. I guess it didn't surprise me. Everything got around Roosevelt, even the most trivial gossip.

Roosevelt's school newspaper, *The Eagle Beagle,* comes out every Friday. It's given out free, and you can usually find a copy strewn around somewhere during the day on Friday.

This particular Friday edition had a little item on the Bible Club and the budding controversy. I was flabbergasted. There was a quote from "Bible Club founder Elaine Cimons" in the story. Elaine said how hopeful she was there could be more meetings in the future, how it was good for everyone to have such a club.

There was also a quote from one of the teachers who'd been at the first club meeting. It must have been the hawk lady, I figured. Her name was Miss Abigail "Abby" Tucker.

"These kids can't hold a Bible study at Roosevelt. We can't have organized religion invading our public school system. It's morally unethical and repugnant. It's also a violation of our constitutional rights," said Abby Tucker.

Yikes. I had *no* idea that's what we were doing. And here I thought Miss Tucker was violating my constitutional right to express my religion. Now she was telling me I was getting in her way. Truly amazing what people will tell newspaper reporters.

Miss Tucker also vowed to bring the full force of the teachers' union in if she had to. Great, I thought. That would be a whole lot of fun. Maybe they'd picket the school or something, taunt us as we forced our way through the lines to get to our little club.

I think Miss Tucker was overreacting. Just a little. But that's life, I guess. Some people just have to have something to fight about. It's what makes them get up in the morning. If they don't have anger, they don't have anything at all.

We all gathered in the principal's outer office just before lunchtime on Friday—Rob, Evan, Elaine, and me. The other kids decided just to let us try Kamber again. We might have better luck with a small group, we all decided.

We didn't say much as we waited. I could see that the secretaries were looking at us curiously. They both had a copy of *The Eagle Beagle* on their desks, and I was quite certain they'd seen the article. I sort of felt like a leper, for some reason.

When the secretary finally ushered us into Kamber's office, I could see that he had a copy of *The Eagle Beagle* open on his desk also. Oh well. That would make things a little more complicated.

"Nice quote, Miss Cimons," Kamber said, glancing down at the newspaper as we filed in.

Elaine blushed. "The reporter just sort of found me in the hallway this week," she mumbled.

"How did the newspaper hear about the story, anyway?" Kamber glowered.

We all glanced at each other. Everybody shrugged, so I knew it wasn't any of us who'd told them.

"I don't think they know," Rob said evenly.

Kamber's eyes locked onto Rob's. They stared at

each other, sizing each other up. Neither backed down. I could see that we were definitely going to have some fun.

"So have we reached a decision?" Kamber asked, settling down into his chair. "If you've brought a lawyer with you, I guess I can presume that you aren't willing to stop meeting?"

"I don't think—" Rob said.

"I'd like to hear from the kids first, if you don't mind!" Kamber snapped.

"I'm speaking for them," Rob said.

"I would very much *like* to hear from them," Kamber insisted.

Rob glanced at us. We'd already decided to let Rob do the talking. "Mr. Ritter speaks for all of us," Elaine said finally.

Kamber clasped his hands. "So. I see. It's going to be like that, is it? Well, then I guess that changes things immensely." He got up out of his chair and walked over to the doorway. "Tina!" he called out. "Come in here! I'll need someone to take minutes on this meeting. Officially."

One of the secretaries hurried into the room and sat down in a chair off to the side as unobtrusively as possible. She held her pen over a notebook, poised to take notes.

"I really don't think we need to get quite this formal yet," Rob said.

"Oh, I think we do," Kamber said.

Rob nodded. "Okay, then, I'd like to open this meeting with an offer. Let the kids hold their Bible Club, and we won't press this any further."

"You don't have a leg to stand on," Kamber laughed. "You don't have a case to press. The club's charter is still under consideration in this office, and the club can't meet until I've ruled on the charter."

"And when exactly, will you do that?" Rob asked.

"These things take time," Kamber said. "I'll have to review it. I may ask for outside consultation. I can't say how long it will be."

"Outside consultation?" Rob asked.

"People or groups who are familiar with this sort of thing," Kamber said evasively.

"You can't tell us how long that will take?" Rob asked.

"No, I can't," Kamber said. "There isn't a deadline for this sort of thing."

"The kids would like to meet while you're reviewing that charter," Rob said.

"Legally, they can't," Kamber said with just the hint of a smile. "The club cannot legally meet on the school grounds until I've formally ruled on the charter."

"And if they try to meet?" Rob asked.

"I wouldn't advise them to try that," Kamber almost growled. "I wouldn't advise them to do that at all."

"But if they do?" Rob persisted.

"Then I may be forced to take legal action," Kamber vowed. "Or even have them arrested."

"On what grounds?" Rob asked.

"Unlawful entry or something like that," Kamber said. "The simple fact of the matter is that, until I've ruled on their charter, it is illegal for them to try to meet. So I would advise them not to do anything foolish."

Rob rose from his chair. "I guess this meeting's over. I would advise *you* to review that charter with all due haste, Mr. Kamber. If not, I may be forced to ask a judge to move the review along."

"I wouldn't do that if I were you, Mr. Ritter," Kamber said mysteriously. "It might be bad for your business."

Rob clenched his hands. It was the only outward sign that he was angry. "You let me worry about my own business, if you don't mind. I'm representing a client here, and the rest of my business is none of your concern."

"It was only advice," Kamber said.

"Well, it's advice I don't need," Rob said. "Now, again, please review that charter as quickly as you can."

"Oh, I will," Kamber said. "But make sure you tell your *clients* that they are not to meet again while it's under review."

"But—" Elaine tried to say.

Rob held up a hand. "We'll discuss that later, Elaine. Not here."

I could see that Elaine was clearly frustrated, but she held her tongue. Just barely.

"Nice meeting you," Kamber said, extending a hand.

"My pleasure," Rob said, taking the hand.

I wondered if it was always like this with adults. You may be seething on the inside, but on the outside, you're syrupy and polite when you shake hands.

Is that what it means to grow up, that you learn how to be nice to those whom you absolutely detest or can't trust? Does it work that way? What would happen if you went around and told everyone exactly what you thought of them all the time?

Most likely, you'd have no friends left. Only enemies.

"That was a complete waste of time," Evan said as we picked up our things in the outer office.

"Not entirely," Rob said. "We now know exactly where Kamber stands."

"And where's that?" Elaine frowned.

Rob glanced over at the remaining secretary, who was pretending not to pay any attention to us.

"Kamber intends to hold onto that charter for as long as he can, which he believes will effectively keep you from meeting. That puts the ball back in our court."

"So what do we do now?" I asked.

"Well, we have two choices," Rob said. "We can either file a lawsuit against the school and try to have it resolved through the court system, or we can take it to the school board."

"Nope, there's a third option too," Evan said.

"What's that?" Elaine asked.

"You—we—can try to meet again. Force the issue. Let it go public, so everybody knows exactly what's going on. Kamber might be forced to back off," Evan said.

Rob nodded. "Actually, I hadn't thought of that as an option. But, as your attorney, I would have to advise you against that course of action because it's illegal. You'd be on school property when you weren't supposed to be, which is trespassing. I can only advise you to take one of the two legal courses of remedy."

"We can still do one of those," Evan persisted. "Either file the lawsuit or go to the school board."

"Or both," I added.

"Yes, we could do both," Rob said.

"But we could also try to meet again, force a confrontation," Evan said.

"Which I can't comment on as your attorney," Rob said.

"We aren't asking you to, Rob," said Evan. "We'll make that decision ourselves. Then we'll let you know."

15

I couldn't believe it. But there it was, right on page D3 of our local newspaper, *The Washington Post.*

"Principal Blocks Bible Study," said the headline on the story in Monday's newspaper. The story was very similar to the one that had appeared in *The Eagle Beagle.* Somebody—a parent, most likely—must have sent *The Eagle Beagle* story to them.

In fact, the *Post* story had the same quotes from Elaine and Abby Tucker, attributed to a "published article on the raging controversy." It was a raging controversy? How had it become that?

But the story also took everything just a little farther. It said that the next scheduled meeting of the Bible Club was this Wednesday, and it was "uncertain" whether the rebel students—I guess that was us—would try to force their way into the classroom.

We'd all talked about it over the weekend, of course. Back and forth, back and forth. That's how our arguments had gone.

Sheryl had wanted to storm the place, naturally. Her personality was like her clothes—big, billowy, and loud. She always wanted to fight about everything with everybody.

Meanwhile, Barry wanted to sue. Jason, surprisingly, was in Sheryl's corner and thought we should just try to hold a club and see what happened. Elaine wanted to wait until Kamber decided on the charter.

And me? What did I want? I was kind of desperately wishing I'd never gotten involved, to be perfectly honest. This whole thing was getting way out of hand. And now, with the story in the newspaper, it was only going to get worse.

My mom came to the rescue, fortunately. It turned out there was another option none of us had thought of.

"I'll bring it up at the PTA meeting Tuesday evening," Mom told me as she was packing us up and sending us off to school Monday morning. "See if I can't get a few parents stirred up."

"Is that a good idea?" I asked her.

"Sure, why not? What harm can it do?"

"It might get people even madder about it all, I guess."

"Madder than they already are?"

"That's true. Everybody's pretty bent out of shape as it is."

"Let me give it a try, Cally," Mom said. "You never know."

True, but somehow, I had the sinking feeling that all of this was only going to get worse before it got better.

16

The school buzzed for two days about the Bible Club. Elaine had become an overnight celebrity in the school. Everybody wanted to talk to her. I mean, she'd been *quoted* in the newspaper. She was famous.

Well, not exactly, but close enough. Closer than I wanted to get to that kind of recognition.

Actually, I felt extraordinarily lucky. No one really knew I was involved in all of this, which I considered a fortunate break. I watched the mobs descend on Elaine during Monday and Tuesday, and I was delighted that it was her and not me.

Elaine kept threatening to bring me into the picture by referring to me as cofounder of the club. I told her that if she did that, I would do something truly horrible to her. She just laughed and kept right on talking to every student who came her way.

Elaine, I have to say, was in pure heaven over the way things were turning out. It wasn't that she liked all the attention. Oh, I'm sure she didn't mind it. Being a celebrity, I mean. But that wasn't what was making her happy.

Elaine was excited because the controversy was propelling so many kids into her path. And each and every one of those kids got a little lesson on the Gospel and what was in the Bible, why it was important to talk about it, etc., etc.

For Elaine, there was nothing sweeter. She could preach endlessly, given the chance. And boy, did she have the chance now. So she was making use of her big opportunity to tell kids about God. Not many were listening, of course. But Elaine didn't care. She just felt like she had to try.

"I'll just plant as many seeds as I can," she told me once. "God will make them grow. My job is just to plant them."

Sometimes, sort of quietly and to myself, I wondered who the gardener was supposed to be. Planting the seeds seemed to be the easy part, if you ask me. I would never tell Elaine that, but I did wonder a little who was supposed to make those seeds grow and sprout into something.

Anyway, I figured that everything would die down by the end of the day on Tuesday.

Wrong. It only got worse.

The reason, I think, was that a rumor swept through the school that we were going to try to meet on Wednesday and that all sorts of weird things were going to happen.

I even heard one kid whisper that *he'd* heard the state police were going to show up and block our way into the classroom.

There was also the PTA meeting Tuesday night, and somehow the word had gotten out that the Bible Club was going to come up at that meeting. Both Elaine and Jason told me some kids were planning to go to it with their parents.

"So is your mom really planning to talk about it at the PTA tonight?" Elaine asked me after fourth period.

I sighed. "That's what she says."

Elaine clenched her fist. "Great! Maybe if we can get some of the parents helping us—"

"Elaine, I don't think it'll work that way," I said quickly.

"What do you mean?"

"I think most of the parents will yell about having a Bible Club at the school," I said glumly.

"Why do you say that?"

"I just think they will, that's all. I don't know why."

"Cally, you never know. We can pray that it will be different. Will you do that? Pray with me that God will make His voice known tonight?"

I looked to my right and left. "Right here in school?" I asked nervously.

"Sure. Why not?"

I stared at Elaine in faint horror. She didn't mind doing this kind of stuff in public at all. It made me unbelievably nervous.

"Elaine, I'll pray about it. I promise," I said quickly. "Anyway, I have to get to class." I edged away.

"Promise?" Elaine called out after me.

"I promise," I called back and then hurried away.

You know, it was funny about stuff like that. Praying in public places, I mean. Elaine and I were so different on some things. And praying in public was one of them.

The way I looked at it was like this. In the Bible, Jesus went off by Himself when He prayed to His Father. He didn't do it publicly, where all the world could see what He was doing.

He didn't make any secret of what He believed in, and He talked constantly about the kingdom of God. But what He didn't do was pray in public.

In fact, I was kind of shocked when I read through the famous Sermon on the Mount. One part of that sermon talks about how you're not supposed to pray on street corners, where you can be seen by men.

No, Jesus said, you were supposed to go into your room, shut the door, and pray to your Father who is in secret.

I guess that's kind of the way I looked at it. I liked to talk to God in private. That's how I prayed.

Elaine was different. She liked to let it all hang out in public, where everyone could see. Nothing was held back. I admired her for that. I felt, in a way, that she had more courage than I did.

And then there was my mom, who took the middle path. She didn't pray in public, but she was also not afraid to talk about what she believed. Like tonight. She'd really go after the PTA, if I knew my mom. They'd never know what hit 'em.

17

"You ready, Cally?" Mom called up the stairs after dinner.

"Just a sec!" I yelled from my room.

"We don't want to be late," Mom yelled back. "Not tonight."

"I know, Mom. I'll be there. I just want to change shirts."

I flumped my head back down on my pillow on the top bunk. The absolute *last* thing in the world I wanted to do was go to this PTA meeting. The closer it got to the time to leave, the worse I felt.

I'd thought about skipping it, just letting Mom go to it by herself. But I knew that wasn't right. She was fighting my fight. The least I could do was go stand there by her side.

Something soft bonked against my head. I reached over without looking up and grabbed the folded socks and blindly threw them back at Chris. The socks thudded against the wall harmlessly.

"Missed," Chris said.

"I won't the next time."

"How'd you get sucked into all of this, anyway?" Chris asked. "Was it that Elaine girl? Did she do this?"

"Yeah, it was her. This whole mess was her idea."

"Should have known," Chris said. "She's sorta

weird, you know it? Just a little off the wall."

"Yeah, I know," I sighed. "But she's nice. And she really wants to do the right thing. You know what I mean?"

Chris laughed. "Sounds like you, birdbrain. You're always getting into messes because of what you believe."

I took a deep breath. "This is going to be bad tonight. I just know it is."

"Ah, don't sweat it so much. Mom is cool about stuff like this. She'll do it up right."

"You're right," I nodded. "Mom does know what she's doing."

Which was interesting to think about, you know. It wasn't so long ago, down in Alabama, before we moved, that Mom had been cowering in front of our lunatic father.

Now, she was bold and brave and daring. She had the world by the tail. She was finishing her college education. She had a great, new job. The family was in pretty good shape.

"Cally James! Get down here right now!" Mom yelled quite loudly.

"Coming!" I yelled back and hopped off the bed like somebody had stuck me with a fork.

"Say hi to Elaine for me," Chris teased as I began to leave.

I stopped long enough to smack Chris and then bolted from the room before he could return the blow. Another pair of socks ricocheted harmlessly down the stairs as I descended them three at a time.

* * * * * * * *

I couldn't believe it. We walked into the gym at

Roosevelt, and the place was like a circus.

The seats were crammed with people. There were four television camera crews set up about twenty feet or so in front of the speakers' podium. There were reporters wandering around the noisy crowd, interviewing people.

Elaine was being interviewed, on camera, by one of the TV reporters as we walked in. I could see that Elaine was talking a mile a minute.

I looked around the crowd as we came in. I spotted both the hawk lady and the tweed jacket guy who'd disrupted our Bible Club. They were seated and ready for tonight's fun festivities.

"Is it usually this jammed?" I asked Mom.

"No, it isn't," Mom said.

"So what's the deal?"

Mom gave me a strange look, as if I'd lost my mind. "You can't be serious, Cally? Surely you know why all these people are here tonight, don't you?"

"Well, yeah, I guess I do. To talk about the Bible Club," I said nervously.

"It's more than that, Cally. You've struck a raw nerve," Mom said, her voice deadly serious. "This debate goes right to the very heart of what's tearing at America's public school system."

"What do you mean?"

"I mean, this is all about what kind of moral values are preached at kids in public schools, and why so many parents choose to send their kids to private schools."

"Kids go to private schools because of Bible Clubs?" I asked, confused.

"No, what I mean is, a lot of parents send their kids to private Christian schools because they like the religious values taught there, as well as the education.

They don't trust the values being taught in the public schools."

"And that's what this is all about, here, tonight?"

"A lot of that, yes," Mom nodded. "This is all about who has control over the moral values taught to our children, and what that teaching is all about."

I have to be honest. I wasn't at all sure I understood what my mother was talking about. The way I looked at it, school was a place you had to go. You did your best to learn about math and science and social studies. But, mostly, it was something you had to endure.

Oh, there was some fun to it. You could play sports and hang out with kids between classes. You made some friends at school. But it wasn't the place I'd choose to go to if I had spare time on my hands, that's for sure.

I'd never thought about it from the teachers' perspective before. At least, not until now. Why were the teachers there at school? What did they get out of all of this? And why were they so threatened by our harmless little Bible Club?

Mom and I took our seats as close to the podium as we could manage. It really was crowded, and loud, in the gym. Everybody in the whole place was talking, all at once.

Elaine caught my eye just as I was taking my seat. The TV reporter had just finished interviewing her, and she was looking around the crowd. She waved at me to come join her. I shook my head. She waved at me again.

When I didn't get up, Elaine marched over. I cringed in my seat. I cringed even lower when I saw that a second TV reporter was hurrying to catch up with Elaine as she was walking toward me.

"Cally!" Elaine called out when she was a few feet

away. "I need some help with these reporters."

"Ah, you can do it, Elaine," I said, my voice raspy.

"Come on, it's fun," Elaine said, beaming from ear to ear. She was really flying. I could see that. She loved all of this. It was a show made just for her.

"Nah, it's OK. You do it," I said.

The TV reporter, a nice-looking lady in a suit, arrived just then. Elaine turned to face her.

"Are you Elaine Cimons?" the reporter asked.

"Yes," Elaine said.

"The founder of the Bible Club?" the reporter asked.

"Yes, the cofounder," Elaine said, a funny smirk on her face. "The other cofounder is right here."

Both Elaine and the reporter turned to me at the exact, same moment. I was certain my face was turning a deep crimson.

"And who are you?" the reporter asked me.

"Cally James," Elaine answered proudly. "He's famous, you know."

"Famous?" the reporter asked. "How so?"

"He won the national indoor tennis championship last winter, for the twelve-and-under division," Elaine said.

I wanted to murder Elaine. I couldn't believe she was doing this to me. I absolutely couldn't believe it.

The TV reporter looked back at me with renewed interest. "Really? You did that?"

I nodded meekly. Mom gave me a friendly squeeze on my elbow and leaned over to whisper in my ear. "Go on, Cally. Elaine needs your help. It'll be all right."

I tried not to slump in my seat. I'd been hoping I could just sit quietly and watch tonight. Fat chance. Nothing ever works the way you think it will.

"Could I interview both of you?" the reporter asked.

"Would that be possible?"

"Oh, sure," Elaine answered. "No problem."

They looked at me. I glanced at Mom once, then got out of my seat slowly. "Okay," I mumbled.

The reporter nodded once, crisply, and then signaled her producer to turn on the camera and lights. She stepped to the side briskly and thrust a padded microphone into our faces.

"I've interviewed a number of parents so far this evening, and they're all quite upset at the way the two of you are disrupting the school. Why are you doing this?" The reporter moved the microphone closer to both of us.

"I don't think we're disrupting the school," Elaine frowned. "We just want to have a Bible Club."

"But these parents I've talked to say you're imposing your own narrow moral values on their children. And they don't like it," the reporter said, and then thrust the microphone back in our faces.

"But we're not imposing anything on anyone," Elaine protested. "The Bible Club is open to anyone who wants to come."

The reporter turned to me. "Do you agree with that, Cally? Aren't you upset by the fact that so many parents see your Bible Club as a disturbing force in your school, a somewhat radical element?"

A sudden calm came over me. It was a good thing too, because I'd been real close to the edge of sheer panic as I watched the reporter go ballistic on us.

"The First Amendment of the Constitution is about freedom of religion," I said, gazing intently at the reporter and not the camera. "And that's all our Bible Club is about. We think we have the right to express ourselves."

"Even if it harms others? Even if, as some parents

allege, you are infringing on the rights of others?"

"That's what this country is all about," I said, wondering where my words were coming from. "We all have the right to talk about what we believe. No one has to listen to us. But we can still talk about it. The Bible Club is just like that. Some of us wanted to meet and talk about things. We have the right to do that. The Constitution says we do."

"But on school grounds?" the reporter asked. "In a building paid for by the taxpayers?"

"I don't think the Constitution says anything about *where* you can talk about religion, or anything else."

"Cally's right," Elaine added. "Freedom of religion isn't just about churches. If you're free to talk about religion and God in this country, that means you can talk about it anywhere. Even in school."

The reporter was about to ask another question, but the PTA president began to pound her gavel to start the meeting. The producer switched off the TV lights, and the reporter thanked us. She was clearly unsatisfied though, and would undoubtedly seek us out after the meeting. Hopefully, I'd be long gone by the time she tried to find us.

The PTA president was a short, rotund woman, with a slightly red face, hair piled high on her head, and a frilly dress that billowed as she talked. And, oh, how she talked. Rapid-fire. So fast you could barely keep up with the torrent of words.

"Who *is* she?" I whispered to Mom.

"Her name is Wilma Baker," Mom whispered back. "She's been here forever. I think she's had five kids come through Roosevelt."

I looked at the others seated on the podium. Kamber was up there. So was the hawk lady, along with two other women I didn't recognize.

Wilma Baker pounded her gavel, calling the meeting to order again. "Let's go, folks!" she barked out. "We have a full agenda this evening. Take your seats, please. And listen up."

A hushed silence settled on the crowd eventually. Wilma waited for it to quiet just a little more. "Good. Now, as you all know, our principal, John Kamber, is up here with us tonight. He'd like to address the PTA first, before we take up the first item on the agenda."

I glanced at Mom. A deep frown creased her face. She hadn't expected this. But Kamber was smart. I guess he figured if he got up and spoke first, he'd set the tone for the meeting. It would go his way.

"Good evening, folks," Kamber said somberly as he stepped up to the microphone. "I'll be brief. I just wanted to update you on something that I'm sure you've all heard about."

Just then, Kamber looked out over the crowd. His eyes swept over the sea of people and somehow settled on me. We looked at each other for the longest moment, before Kamber moved on. I felt as if he were speaking directly to me.

"I'm talking about the advent of a very disturbing, troubling phenomenon in our school—the formation of a so-called Bible Club at Roosevelt," he continued.

"Now, I'm sure these kids mean well. I know they just want to meet and talk about something *they* believe in. The problem, however, is that they are not just an island unto themselves, as all of you know. Their actions affect others. They are infringing on the rights of others.

"What of the Muslims at the school, and the Jews, and the others who do not believe in their religion and have their own religious beliefs? They are offended by a Christian Bible Club. It is not their Bible Club. They are forbidden from entering such a club.

"And there is the problem, folks. Because they cannot enter such a club, because it is so alien to their own beliefs and because its presence angers them, it is a force for harm in our school. It is a disrupting force.

"If I—or, I should say, we at Roosevelt—allow such a club at Roosevelt, we run the risk of sanctifying and glorifying such activity. *We,* in effect, establish a state religion, of sorts. And that, my friends, is clearly forbidden by the Constitution.

"So I come to you with a heavy heart this evening. As much as I'd like to be able to allow all different kinds of activities at Roosevelt, I really cannot permit such an activity as this at our school. I'm sure all of you understand what I'm saying. I hope you support my efforts."

I could see that my mom was fuming. In fact, as Kamber was winding up his arguments, my mom started to fidget in her seat. Finally, she could take it no longer. She jumped from her seat and strode up to a microphone that was set up in the audience.

Mom grabbed the microphone and tried to say something. No one could hear her. She reached down and flipped a switch. A screech echoed through the hall briefly. "Is this on?" she asked. Her voice boomed out across the audience.

Wilma Baker rose in her seat and said something. Mom just ignored her and addressed Kamber. "That's all a bunch of nonsense, you know," she said. The crowd stirred a little.

"I beg your pardon?" Kamber asked.

"What the kids are trying to accomplish with their little Bible Club is no more radical or controversial than what other students are doing in the chess club or the glee club. And it's hardly establishing a state religion. They just want to meet and talk. That's all."

"But Mrs. James," Kamber said patiently, "surely, you realize that their club is an affront to all of those who *don't* believe as they do. If I allow them to meet at Roosevelt, then I sanction their activity."

"No, you don't," Mom said sharply. "You tolerate it. Just as the Constitution allows. It says that government will tolerate the expression of religion, not try to stop it at every turn. That's what freedom of religion is. Allowing people to talk about their God-given rights."

There was a smattering of applause in the crowd. But most of the crowd was stirring, and in the other direction, I think.

"The Constitution clearly says that there is supposed to be a clear separation of Church and State," Kamber said. "And if we allow this kind of activity to go on at Roosevelt, then we breach that separation."

"Mr. Kamber," Mom said. "If you'd read the Constitution, you'd know that what it says is that the state will not pass any laws establishing a religion. That's all it says."

"Taxpayer money would be spent on their Bible Club, I'm afraid," Kamber said. "And that means the state would be sanctioning their activity."

"It's *supposed* to allow the kids to meet," Mom answered back. "The Constitution allows people to express themselves. The First Amendment allows free speech, and it also allows freedom of religion. If the kids want to have a Bible Club, then they ought to be able to."

"But what about all those kids who don't believe as they do?" Kamber questioned. There were quite a few heads bobbing in the audience at that question. I could see that Mom was clearly outnumbered here.

"Then they can have their own clubs—the Koran Club, the Torah Club, the Whatever Club," Mom said. "I don't care. None of us here should care. All that really matters is that we protect our fundamental rights. And one of them is the right to express our religious beliefs."

"But I'm sorry, Mrs. James," Kamber said. "They just can't do it on school grounds, in a classroom paid for with taxes. That crosses over the line, past the necessary separation of Church and State."

There was another screech in the hall. Another parent had stepped up to the microphone set up on the other side of the gym.

"Look," said a young woman dressed in a business suit. "I don't want my kids exposed to the nonsense this lady is trying to protect. Christianity is a religion of murderers and fools, and I don't want my school preaching that kind of garbage. Not here, not at Roosevelt."

A second, and then a third and a fourth parent lined up behind her. The second parent grabbed the microphone. "Mr. Kamber, I just want to applaud what you're doing. It may not be popular, but you have to keep this kind of thing out of Roosevelt. I'm careful to make sure my kids aren't exposed to the insanity of the organized religions. I don't want that kind of thing creeping into the school system."

The third parent was even more blunt. "Christianity is dead in America. Only ignoramuses believe in it anymore. The enlightened, intelligent community is moving to a higher religion, and that's what I'd like to see Roosevelt aspire to. Not some hulk of a relic, which is what Christianity has become."

The fourth parent stepped up to the microphone.

"That's right. We're entering a New Age. Why in the world would Roosevelt preach Christianity, when it is clearly the wrong way to go? Why not teach our kids something that can really help them, not something that scares them out of their wits with talk of hell and damnation and devils?"

With each successive speaker, the crowd had begun to applaud. By the time the fourth parent had stepped up to oppose my mom, the crowd was roaring its approval. Just then, Mom looked awful small up there at the microphone.

"I didn't come here to start a fight," Mom said, trying to be heard over the commotion. "If you want to start a New Age club at Roosevelt, I would support your child's right to go to one. I may not think it's right, but I would support your child's right to go to one."

"That's not the point, Mrs. James," Kamber interjected. "What is at issue here is whether to allow a Bible Club at Roosevelt. And I think the sentiment is clearly against allowing such a club."

"We don't want it!" a voice called out from the audience.

"Yeah, get out of Roosevelt!" a second voice yelled.

"Send your kid to a private school!" a third yelled.

Wilma Baker quickly stepped up to the podium and banged her gavel to restore order. It didn't do much to silence the growing din.

My mom held up her hand. "Look, all I want to do is protect my child's right to talk about what he believes in. That's all. He has a constitutional guarantee—"

"Not at Roosevelt, he doesn't!" someone else shouted out.

"Yes, he does," Mom countered. "He does have that right."

Then Mom turned and walked back to her seat, ignoring all of the angry glances at her. I was kind of in shock. I hadn't expected such raw anger. People were really angry at us over this Bible Club. I could see that clearly, for the first time.

What had happened to us in America? I found myself wondering. What had happened in our schools, that people would be so angry when you tried to talk about the Bible and God and Jesus Christ?

It was strange. Very strange. The people in that gym were very, very angry about something. I had no idea what they were so angry about. Were they mad at God? At Elaine and me for bringing it up in school? What was it they were so afraid of?

The rest of the evening was a blur to me. More parents got up and denounced us for starting such a club. Only one other parent defended us. She, like my mom, said the Constitution protected our right to talk about God in the public schools.

But the majority was against us. There was no question about that. It was Them against Us, and there weren't very many of Us.

It made me wonder what the rest of the country was like. Was it like this everywhere? Were there millions of parents out there—just like the ones who showed up tonight—who are trying to change the world to fit their own vision and who won't tolerate any interference?

Were there at least some parents out there who silently supported us, who wanted us to be able to talk about God in school but who were afraid of being shouted down?

I hoped so.

18

Mom was so angry on the way home from the PTA she could barely contain herself. She kept gripping the steering wheel so hard I thought she was going to pull it right out of the dashboard.

"What's happened to our country?" she repeated, almost to herself.

"What do you mean, Mom?" I finally asked her.

Mom didn't answer. At least, not right away. I think she was still in shock that so many parents had given her such a hard time.

"You know, Cally, I always thought America was a religious country, that it is a God-fearing country," Mom said.

"Yeah, we have 'In God We Trust' on all our money," I offered.

"Yes, exactly," Mom nodded. "But something has happened. At least, here in Washington, something has happened."

"What? What has happened?"

Mom shook her head sadly. "I think the Christian community—for the first time in America's history—is in the minority. We are a minority."

"What does that make everybody else?" I asked timidly, not sure I wanted to hear her answer.

"I'm not sure, Cally," she answered somberly. "But I'll tell you one thing. It means that the Christian community in America, for the first time in its life, is going to have to fight for its rights. And it must fight very, very hard."

* * * * * * * *

We probably made a zillion phone calls before we decided to risk having our regular Bible Club on Wednesday. Elaine and I finally decided to call every single kid who showed up at the first club to ask them if they'd come to a second. All of them wanted to.

Elaine had also talked to Mrs. Sanders, the teacher who'd let us use her classroom in the first place. She'd thought about it for a long time, Elaine said, and she'd finally decided to let us use her room.

Which meant she would surely be fired. She knew that, she told Elaine, but she'd decided to go ahead anyway.

"Mrs. Sanders said she'll probably try to find a job at a Christian school after she's been fired," Elaine told me in about our seventh telephone conversation Tuesday night.

"Does she really want to do this?" I asked.

"Yeah, she's pretty sure about it," Elaine answered. "She's thought it all through. She doesn't want to teach in a school with a guy like Kamber as principal."

"Can't blame her."

"So how do we do this tomorrow, Cally?" Elaine asked.

"Beats me," I said. "I guess we just show up and see what happens."

"What if there are police?"

I snorted. "No way. There won't be police."

"But what if there are?" Elaine persisted.

"Then we get arrested, I guess."

"And go to jail?"

I thought about that for a second. "Maybe we better ask Rob—Evan's lawyer—to come with us."

"Good idea," Elaine said. "What about Evan? Do you think he'll show up?"

"I don't know," I said. "I'll call him and see. I know he'll call his dad's lawyer for us."

"But will he come to the Bible Club?"

I sighed. "Maybe."

"Cally, does he believe?" Elaine asked.

"I know he believes in us, in what we're doing," I mused. "Beyond that, I don't have a clue."

"You've never asked him about it?"

"Nope. Never. And I'm not sure I could."

"But why not?"

"I, um . . . I don't know," I stammered. "I just don't think I can."

"Cally, Cally, what are you afraid of?" Elaine asked gently.

I don't know, I thought. I really don't know. I wasn't afraid of Evan. I wasn't afraid, really, to talk about God and Jesus Christ. But I couldn't put the two together—talking about God and Jesus Christ to Evan. I don't know why. I just couldn't.

"I'll talk to him, eventually," I told Elaine.

"Get him to come to the Bible Club," Elaine said.

"I'll try," I vowed. "I promise."

I woke up Wednesday morning with a huge headache. I hadn't been able to sleep. I'd tossed and turned the whole night, visions of jail and police dancing through my head.

I couldn't shake the feeling that we were walking into a blizzard. I felt helpless about it too.

We *had* to do this. I knew it. Deep in my heart, I was certain it was the right thing to do, regardless of what the parents had told Mom at the PTA and all the arguments from Kamber about how we were disrupting the school.

I mean, it didn't make any sense. *Why couldn't you talk about God in a public school, for crying out loud? Give me one good reason,* I thought. Every part of me said that we were right, and they were wrong.

If you could talk about sex and drugs and all kinds of other junk in school, why couldn't you talk about God too? Why?

But I knew we were really asking for it, going to the second Bible Club. I knew it, but I felt powerless to do anything about it.

It didn't make it any better when everybody razzed me at breakfast. They'd all seen me on the news the night before. The TV reporter who'd interviewed Elaine and me had used some of it on the air.

I was famous, sort of. I thought I looked like some

dumb, little kid, spouting off about things I didn't understand. But Chris said I looked cool, and Jana said she thought I sounded smarter than everybody else.

I knew they were just saying those things to make me feel a little better. But it was still nice.

"Better wear your makeup, Cally," Chris chuckled at the breakfast table.

"Makeup?" I asked.

"You know," Chris said, giving Jana and Karen a sly, sideways glance. "For your big television appearance today."

I grimaced. "Oh, shut up. I'll bet nobody will be there. We'll just show up and have our little club and that will be that."

Karen started laughing. "Cally, you're crazy. The whole *world* will be there today."

"Yeah, it'll be a mob scene," Chris chimed in. "And you'll be right in the middle of it."

"I don't know," I half-mumbled. "I hope not."

"You can hope all you want," Chris said. "It won't change anything. You hold that Bible Club, and the place is gonna go bananas."

Chris jerked his head around. He always heard things just a little sooner than the rest of us, for some reason. We all heard the grinding gears of the creaking school bus a second later.

"That's yours," Chris said, slamming his chair back. "C'mon, John and Susan, we better get ready. We don't wanna miss our bus the way Cally and the twins are gonna miss theirs."

I almost knocked my chair over getting out of it. Jana and Karen were already packed up. They just had to run upstairs, say good-bye to Mom, and run out the door. I had to gather everything up first, then run to catch up.

I caught the bus just as the doors were closing.

Yet as I walked up the stairs to the bus, I had the funniest feeling. I sort of wished that I'd missed the bus and stayed at home. Everything would have been a whole lot easier and simpler.

20

The off-duty cops didn't show up until sixth period, an hour before school ended. I spotted the first one just hanging out as I was going to my last class.

"How many other cops are here?" I asked him.

"We don't give out operational details like that. Might jeopardize the mission."

I walked away shaking my head. Operational details? The mission? Who were these guys preparing for anyway? We weren't exactly the mafia or drug overlords.

Elaine and I had already decided that we were both going to duck out of our last class early and meet Rob out behind the cafeteria to map out our strategy. We'd just get hall passes for the rest room a few minutes before class ended and not come back.

As I hurried through the empty corridors, I spotted the TV news trucks through one of the windows at the front of the school. So, they were here in full force. I stopped in my tracks, and hurried toward the doors at the front.

Cautiously, I poked my head out the door and peeked around the corner. Sure enough, there were four of those TV trucks out in front of the school. A mob of reporters had gathered in front of the entrance that was closest to Room 122, where our Bible Club would be held.

I was sure they were just waiting for the bell to ring so they could bolt inside and set up. A huge knot began to tighten in my stomach.

I closed the door and hurried on my way, determined not to think about what would likely happen in a few minutes.

Elaine and Rob were waiting for me when I arrived.

"What took you so long?" Elaine asked. "School's almost over."

"I stopped to see what was going on near Mrs. Sanders' room," I said.

"What?" Elaine asked. "What's happening?"

"The place is crawling with reporters," I grimaced. "And I've seen cops all over the school too."

Rob shook his head. "Your principal has certainly covered all the bases. You sure you guys want to go ahead with this?"

Elaine nodded. "I'm sure. We have to."

Rob turned to me. "How about you?"

I didn't hesitate. "Yes, I'm sure. Let's do it."

Rob glanced back and forth between the two of us. "This is brave of you, both of you. I know it isn't easy, having to confront something like this."

"The others are brave too," Elaine added. "They're all willing to do this."

The school bell rang. We all jumped a little. "Hey, we'd better hustle over to the room."

We walked back into the school briskly, working our way through the throng of students who were hurrying to leave school and get home to more important things.

When we got to the classroom, my heart sank. It was impossible. I could see that in an instant.

There was a wall of three imposing looking policemen standing in front of the entrance to Room 122.

The media were off to the side, all gathered up and poised for action. I counted at least fifteen reporters.

I looked around the hallways. The members of our Bible Club were beginning to arrive. They were leaning against the wall or hanging out in pairs in the other doorways, talking softly. Some of the other students were drifting by to see what was going on.

Within a few minutes, quite a crowd had gathered. They were all waiting to see what was going to happen. Elaine, Rob, and I stepped off to one side.

"I want to try to go in," Elaine whispered fiercely.

"I'm going with you then," I said.

"I have to advise you against it," Rob warned. "You will probably be arrested."

"I don't care," Elaine said. "We have to."

I looked at the other kids. "Let's tell the others what we're going to do."

"Good idea," Elaine nodded. We both began to signal to Barry, Jason, Sheryl, and the others to join us. They began to drift over. I noticed then, that Lisa Collins was here, but that Evan hadn't shown up. I'd have to think about that later.

"Cally and I are going to try to go in," Elaine told the group when we were all gathered.

"But you can't get through those cops," Barry said.

"We have to try," Elaine said.

"You'll only get arrested," Jason said, glancing nervously over his shoulder.

"It's the only thing we can do," Elaine persisted. "We have to do something. Otherwise, Kamber wins and we have to disband our club."

"I think we should all go," Sheryl said, looking around at the other club members to see if they agreed. There were a few halfhearted nods of approval.

"Yeah," Barry added. "They can't arrest all of us, can they?"

I started laughing. "Sure, they can. Jails are pretty big places. They hold a lot of people."

The crowd gathered around Room 122 was big, now. It had to be at least 100 or so. The whole place was buzzing with anticipation.

Elaine started to edge toward the room. "I don't care if I'm arrested. We have to try. Who's going with me?"

Sheryl stepped forward immediately. Barry hesitated only for an instant, but then joined her. I let out a big sigh and moved forward as well. We all looked back at Jason.

"Oh, why not," Jason sighed.

We all hesitated for just a couple of seconds more. "Anyone else want to come along?" Elaine asked.

Two more kids stepped forward—Henry Westin, a boy who was a good six inches shorter than the rest of us, and Joan Barrett, a thin girl who wore glasses so thick she had to wear a band to keep them on her head.

"Great, Joanie and Henry," Elaine said. "Anyone else? Okay, then, let's go face the lions."

We all began to walk forward toward the classroom. There was a sudden stillness in the air as the crowd that had gathered held its collective breath. The cameras gathered outside the entrance to the classroom all came to life, filming the great event.

"Hey, kids!" one of the reporters shouted as we neared the doorway. "Got a statement?"

I glanced at Elaine. She just shrugged. "Why not?" she whispered. "It can't hurt now."

We all sort of veered off toward the cameras as a group. Sheryl was holding on to Joanie's hand for support. Not a bad idea, I thought.

Boom microphones were thrust out as we approached the throng of reporters. Red lights blinked on the cameras. Pens were poised over notebooks.

"Why are you doing this?" a reporter asked.

"Because we want to hold our club, that's why," Elaine said immediately, answering for the group.

"But what about the separation of church and state?" another reporter asked.

"The Constitution doesn't say anything about not talking about God in school," I said. "It just says the state can't, you know, establish a religion."

"But isn't that what the state — what Roosevelt — would be doing if it let you hold this club?" the second reporter followed up.

"We just want to talk about God," Sheryl said in a very small voice. "What's so wrong about that?"

"Why don't all of you just leave and go to one of those private *Christian* schools?" a third reporter asked, her voice dripping with sarcasm and scorn. And I thought reporters were supposed to just cover the news — not make fun of people. So much for that theory.

"We don't want to go to a private school," Sheryl said. "We want to go to Roosevelt."

"My folks can't afford a private school," Barry spoke up.

"You still haven't answered the first question," another reporter said. "Why are all of you doing this? Why are you causing so much trouble?"

I could feel myself starting to get angry, like I did in a close tennis match when I wasn't playing well. Usually in those matches, I just started rushing the net like a madman to get rid of whatever was ailing me. Too bad there wasn't a net in sight here.

"Elaine *did* answer your question," I said loudly, addressing the first reporter who'd asked the question. "We want to hold our club. It's as simple as that. No big deal. Anyone can understand that."

"But why? You haven't said *why?*" the reporter said.

The whole group of reporters instinctively surged forward just a little, waiting for the kill shot.

That amazing, peaceful, settling calm descended on me. I knew who had arrived to bail me out, just in the nick of time. "There is no reason God should not be a part of Roosevelt, part of a public school," I said quietly.

"The Constitution was written to protect my right to talk about God and Jesus Christ—here, in church, in the park, on the street. The Constitution *protects* my right to express my religion and my faith in God. It doesn't separate me or my faith from the school, or anywhere else for that matter."

I had no idea where those words came from, of course. I was certain they weren't entirely from me. I was never quite that thoughtful. But, boy, was I glad God had arrived to help me out.

I remembered then, that this was one of His many promises in the Bible. That when you are surrounded by your accusers, He will help you out with the words you will need for your defense.

"That's all you want?" another reporter said. "Just to talk about God in school?"

"That's all," Elaine said. "Nothing more. We just want to talk about Him. It isn't like this is a war or anything."

"It's a war of words," a reporter from behind the cameras called out.

There was some murmuring from the crowd that

was continuing to press forward for a glimpse of our little, impromptu press conference. I glanced over and saw the crowd part to let Kamber through.

"Let's break all this up!" Kamber bellowed, sweeping his hand through the air. No one budged, of course. They weren't about to miss this.

Kamber strode up to the cameras and our group. We all stood very still, not sure what to do or expect now.

"Let's go," Kamber said, looking at all of us. "This is quite enough. You can all leave now that you've had your fun."

"We're not doing this for fun, Mr. Kamber," Elaine said bravely. "We just want to hold our Bible Club."

"Well, you aren't holding it *here* at Roosevelt, I can assure you of that, young lady," Kamber said grimly. "Now, let's move this sideshow out of here."

Elaine glanced over at me. If we didn't do something, right now, we would lose whatever momentum we'd gathered. She jerked her head toward the doorway to Room 122, where the three burly cops were still waiting patiently. They hadn't moved a muscle during our press conference.

I nodded. Elaine and I broke toward the door at the same time. The others followed our lead and trailed behind. We were at the doorway before Kamber could step in front of us. I could hear, but not see, all the reporters and camera crews scurrying to catch up to us.

"We'd like to go in, please," Elaine addressed one of the cops in the nicest, sweetest voice she could muster.

"Not in here, little lady," one of the cops said.

"Please, would you just move aside so we can go in?" Elaine said again.

"If you try to enter this room, we will arrest you," a

second cop said in a flat, emotionless voice. "This is not an approved activity, so all of you are trespassing."

Elaine grabbed my hand. I held it tight. We took two steps forward and tried to walk between two of the cops.

Rough hands seized both of my arms. Elaine was pulled from my grasp. There were a few gasps and shouts from the crowd. The cameras pressed in close, capturing every moment.

"Hey, that hurts," Elaine said. I glanced over at her. Her face was a mask of pain. It about broke my heart to see her this way.

Four more policemen materialized out of thin air. I couldn't help but admire how well prepared Kamber had been for this. He'd covered all the bases.

We were whisked through the crowd by two of the cops. I glanced over my shoulder to see that the other cops were also dragging the other five kids along as well. They'd arrested all seven of us. The gang of seven. It was almost funny.

They pushed Elaine and me into the back of a big wagon. The others arrived shortly after that. We all took our seats, and then two cops slid in beside us. They didn't say a word. They just sat there like mummies as the van started up and began to move out.

I looked out the window. A camera was thrust up to the window just at that very moment. Great, I thought. That's what will be on the news tonight—a nice picture of my ugly mug as we were being dragged off to jail.

Oh well, I thought. It could have been worse. I could have said something really stupid to go along with just how dumb and wretched I felt at this very moment.

----②①

Actually, I was wrong. It wasn't just the picture of me being carted away in the police van they showed over and over on the TV news.

They also kept showing me talking about the freedom of religion, where I spouted off that you ought to be able to talk about God anywhere you felt like.

I was still numb with shock when Mom came down and got me from the holding room at the police station. I don't even know what I'd been charged with. Talking about God on land paid for with taxes?

Rob stayed with all of us the whole time. He'd followed us to the police station, and he'd argued forcefully with the cops throughout the whole process.

I couldn't hear all of what Rob was saying, but it was plain enough. He was arguing that we were just kids, caught up in something bigger than us. He was also arguing that all the charges should just be dropped so this thing could go to court.

In the end, Rob won. The police dropped all the charges against us, with only a warning not to pull another stunt. But the damage had been done. There was no turning back now.

We were all exhausted when our parents came to pick us up. Before we all left though, Rob held a meeting to see what we wanted to do next. Surprisingly, no one wanted to quit.

"I say, take Kamber to court!" Sheryl half yelled.

"Yeah, we can win," Barry added.

Rob looked at all of us somberly. Then he looked up at the waiting parents, who were gathered around us as well. I looked up at Mom.

"I think it's up to the kids," said Jason's father, a well-dressed, middle-aged man. "If this is something they believe in, something they want to fight for then I think we ought to let them have their day in court."

Jason's dad was clearly speaking for the other parents. There were nods of agreement all around the tight circle. My mom was nodding too. I reached up and squeezed her hand. She squeezed back.

"But can we try not to get arrested again?" Barry's mother asked. "We were fortunate this time, but . . ."

"I can assure you that there will not be another incident like this," Rob interjected. "We—the kids— have made their point. I don't think they need to challenge the school's authority over how public property is used. We can argue this out in court."

"So what *is* our next step?" Elaine asked anxiously.

Rob held up a folder. "I have all the papers in here. I'll file them with the court tomorrow. Hopefully, we'll have a chance to argue our case in a matter of days."

"What should we do until then?" asked Henry Westin.

Rob grinned. "Try to stay out of trouble."

"What if we can't?" Sheryl asked.

Rob paused for a moment. "Look. You all need to understand something. You've become public figures, in a way. People will be watching what you do. That means you have to be extra careful, both in what you say and what you do. Does that make sense?"

We all nodded. "Which means," Rob continued, "that you have to avoid trouble at all costs. Let me argue your case for you, in court, where it ought to be argued."

"Do you think this could go to the Supreme Court?" Joanie Barrett asked breathlessly.

Rob smiled. "Oh, I think we're likely to have this resolved one way or another long before that."

"But is there a chance it could go there?" Joanie persisted.

"Oh, sure," Rob shrugged. "There's always that chance, when the case involves Constitutional Law. But, really, we're a long way from anything like that."

When we broke up to go home, we all discovered that our night really hadn't ended. There were more reporters and camera crews waiting for us as we left the police station.

This time, Rob walked up to the reporters and spoke for all of us. I was glad beyond words that he did that. I was sick to death of all the confrontation. I just wanted to go home, fall on my bed, and collapse.

The reporters tried to get around Rob and to us as we were piling into our cars. But Rob was pretty good and persuasive. He was also firm with them, like he was a pro or something at all of this.

A spokesman for the police came out and began talking to the reporters just as the cars all began to leave.

You know, it was funny. I had the awful sense that this whole thing had gotten just a little out of our control, that we'd entered a world where adults argued about things that I didn't completely understand.

I wasn't sure if I liked that or not. But I guess we all have to grow up someday and face things we don't want to. This seemed like one of those days.

22

The next day was totally and completely ridiculous at school. Nobody got any work done. The place was a zoo. The teachers complained all day long.

The story of our confrontation and arrest—with pictures and everything—was all over the front page of *The Washington Post,* big as life.

It also meant that zillions of reporters were now in full, hot pursuit of "the story." It really was pretty funny to watch. Reporters were hanging out around the playground, near the cafeteria, in the parking lot—anywhere they could snag a student to talk to.

And boy, were the students talking. They were talking like crazy, about anything and everything they could think of.

I spied Kamber with a reporter after second period. He was really going to town with the reporter. His jaws were flapping sixty miles an hour. I wondered what the two of them were talking about. How the Constitution was a sacred trust, not to be tread on lightly? Stuff like that?

More likely Kamber was talking about himself and his role in all of this. This was his chance for fame and glory. This was his one, big shot at the brass ring. Do this one right and, who knows, maybe he could go on to become a Supreme Court judge or something. Anything's possible

I avoided reporters all day long. I just didn't have the heart to talk to any of them. The whole thing had somehow gotten muddled and confused along the way. Nobody really cared about the Bible Club anymore. It had gone beyond that, to some bigger fight that I didn't understand.

Why do people get so nervous when you start talking about God and Jesus Christ in public? I mean, I know I'd always been afraid to talk about what I believed to another person. But, if I was asked, I'd talk about it to anyone. I was proud of what I believed in.

There was clearly something going on here that I just didn't understand. There had to be a reason why everyone was going a little nutty over this whole thing.

As the day wore on, I began to keep score. The most visited place by reporters was easily Kamber's office. The reporters trooped in and out of there all day long. I counted at least twenty visits throughout the day.

But Mrs. Sanders was also a popular target. Reporters kept showing up outside Room 122 all day long, trying to pull her aside for a few comments. She was probably late for every one of her classes that day.

I only saw Elaine once during the day, and she was also talking rapidly to reporters, making her case. I was proud of Elaine. She never backed down. Never. She'd fight until the very end.

Elaine waved at me when she saw me, inviting me to come over and talk to the reporter too. I just waved back and shook my head. I really and truly wanted nothing to do with reporters today.

By the time the day ended and tennis practice began, I was exhausted. I was having an almost impossible time paying attention to anything for very long.

Evan was waiting for me. "Saw you on the news last night. You're a superstar," he chided me.

"Hardly," I muttered, wishing he would just drop the subject.

Evan glanced over at the four big vans parked in front of the school, decorated with big letters and numbers signifying the different news channels. "I'll bet they interviewed half the school today," he laughed.

"Just about."

"It really has gotten a little spooky to watch."

"Tell me about it," I said, unzipping my racket cover and bouncing my hand on the strings to make sure the tension was okay.

"You know, Cally, I meant to tell you why I didn't stop by your club yesterday—"

"Hey, no problem," I said quickly. "You don't need to explain."

"Yes, I do. I *want* to tell you."

I looked up at Evan. "Look. Really. You don't have to tell me. It's none of my business."

Evan looked away. "It's not that I don't believe in what you guys are doing. I think what you're doing is great. It's just that . . . that . . ."

"Evan, I know," I said quietly. "You don't have to explain. I know you're still thinking things through, about your life, about who God is. I can see that."

Evan nodded vigorously, like a drowning man who's just been thrown a lifeline. "That's it exactly. I haven't thought it all through, and I felt sort of funny showing up for your Bible Club when I wasn't real sure yet of what I believed."

"So don't sweat it then. Okay?"

"Okay," Evan sighed, glad to get this past him.

"You'll get around to it when it's the right time. I think I know you by now."

"You think?" the old Evan grinned.

"Yeah, I know you well enough to make sure you don't take a game off me today."

Quick as a flash, before I could react, Evan grabbed a ball, flipped it over at me, and bonked it off my head. It rolled away before I could grab it and send it back at him. "Gotcha," he said.

I leaped to my feet. "You'll pay for that. Dearly."

"No way," Evan said. "I'm hot today, and you have other things on your mind. You're all mine today."

23

As he'd promised, Rob filed the lawsuit against Kamber and the school the day after we'd all been arrested, the day the reporters showed up at the school.

Rob said he'd asked the judge for an immediate hearing, and he'd been granted one. The judge planned to hear opening arguments about why he should take the case on Friday, just two days after we'd all been arrested.

Mom let me stay up extra late Thursday night so I could join "the gang of seven" over at Rob's house. We went over strategy. We talked things through.

Rob's argument was pretty simple. The Constitution says the state can't *establish* any one religion or creed. But it also says that the state is supposed to guarantee that anyone can talk freely about their religious beliefs, anywhere they like.

Rob said the facts were pretty clear. The state—in this case, Kamber and Roosevelt—weren't establishing anything. But they were *blocking* us by not letting us talk about God.

It all made sense to me. Sort of. I was glad I wasn't a lawyer. It reminded me of some of the conversations I'd overheard with Mom and her lawyer, when she was talking about getting a divorce from Dad. Stuff about legal rights and who did what when, and what a judge might rule on.

It seemed strange to me that you had to have law-yers and courts for things like this. People should be allowed to talk about what they believe. If no one wants to listen, fine. But you don't need a court to decide what people can talk about, and what they can't.

I didn't sleep much Thursday night. I got dressed up in my very best clothes for the hearing at the court Friday morning.

I don't know how she did it, but somehow Mom got Kamber to agree to let "the gang of seven" out of school Friday morning so we could go to court.

When Mom and I arrived at the court, I couldn't believe it. There were about twenty people standing in front of the court with signs. They were standing there in front of all the TV cameras, doing interviews and bobbing their signs up and down.

I read some of the signs. "Christian, go home," one said. "Keep our public schools pure," said another. "Don't let God in our schools," read a third.

How did these people hear about this? Why were they here? Who would want to give up a day to come and stand outside a courtroom waving a sign?

But then I looked at the little, red lights glowing silently on top of the TV cameras as one after another of the protesters were being interviewed and I under-stood. It made sense.

These people, like the kids at school and like Kamber, wanted to be in the spotlight. They wanted a chance to be "famous." Did the whole world want to be on TV? Was that what this was all about?

Mom and I ducked into the courtroom before any of the reporters could see us, thankfully. We joined the others who were gathered there, just behind the attorneys' benches in the small courtroom.

Kamber was there with three lawyers, it looked like. He was certainly enjoying himself, yucking it up with all of them as they waited for the hearing to begin.

We didn't say much among ourselves as we waited nervously for the judge to enter the courtroom. I don't think any of us were exactly sure what might happen.

When the judge came in, we all stood and then sat uneasily as the proceedings began. I studied the judge for a few moments. He was an older man, with gray hair and a double chin. It was hard to see much else because of the billowing robe he wore.

So this is how hard problems are settled in our country, I thought. This is where it all winds up. In a court. I almost missed the opening discussion because I was daydreaming about how silly it all seemed, trying to argue about God in a court.

Because God isn't stuck in some box. You can't put a boundary or anything like that around Him. This whole thing now seemed so incredibly silly.

No judge, no court, no lawyers, no rules, no police, no protesters could ever truly keep God out of the public schools. God was already there. He'd always been there, speaking quietly and insistently to anyone who would answer His gentle knock at the door.

I listened to Kamber's lawyers make their case that the school had a "duty" to uphold the Constitution and protect the rights of all the other students in the school who did not want to be subjected to the views of our Bible Club.

I listened then, as Rob made his case—that we, the students, simply wanted to express our own religious beliefs, which were also guaranteed by the very same Constitution the other side said forbid us from talking about God at school.

Then we all sat back and waited for the judge to rule. I had no idea what he was supposed to do with this. It was all new to me.

The judge didn't say anything for the longest time. He studied the papers before him for a full five minutes, it seemed, before he finally spoke.

When he looked up, the judge looked squarely at Kamber. The two of them just stared at each other for the longest time. Then the judge turned his gaze on us, "the gang of seven." I had no idea what he was thinking.

I had this funny feeling. My mind started drifting again, thinking about what Judgment Day before God must be like.

Would it be like this—in some kind of a courtroom, with God up at the bench, hearing arguments about how rotten or good you were during your life?

Would Satan be on the other side, accusing you, threatening you, telling God about how horrible you'd been during your life?

But, you know, this was the really neat thing about being a Christian. When you come before God on that day, when God has to decide about your life, you can actually have the best lawyer in the world.

If you ask Jesus Christ to enter your life, He will become your lawyer, your advocate, with His Father on that day. Jesus will argue your case. And what He will tell His Father is that you are sorry for the rotten things you've done, that you want to be forgiven.

I could almost see God pounding His gavel then, ruling on my life. "Forgiven!" He would boom.

I pitied those who did not have Jesus arguing their case. I know I wouldn't want to go up against Satan, trying to defend myself for all the crummy things I'd ever done.

I shook my head and looked up at the bench again. The judge was still shuffling some papers, but I could see he was about to make a ruling.

"I must say," the judge intoned slowly, "that in all my years as a judge, I have never had a case quite like this come before me. Never. And I hope I never will again. This case is truly awful. There can be no other word for it.

"Schools are a place of learning. It is a great honor to be a teacher. It is their job to shape young, eager minds as they search for knowledge. And the search for the meaning of life, why we're here, whether our lives matter or not—that is the deepest, most profound question of all. It is the central question to all learning. There can be no doubt of that.

"What shocks me about this case is that a school would go out of its way to keep one very possible answer to that question—that God exists and shapes the world's events—from even being discussed in school.

"I simply and truly cannot believe that anyone would keep that discussion from happening in school. It makes no sense to me. Learning, and that includes learning about what ultimately gives meaning to everything, is all that is important in school.

"And yet, I am torn by the notion that the Constitution was established in America to protect an individual's rights. It is the only document in the world to absolutely guarantee someone the right to life, liberty, and the pursuit of happiness.

"What I would like to do in this case is guarantee that students have a right to learn, and that includes learning about the nature of God, if He exists, while protecting the individual rights of other students who may not care to ask questions about God.

"That is what I would like to do here, but I have to admit that I have no idea how to go about it. I simply do not know how to answer that question. In fact, I do not believe it can be resolved in a court of law.

"What I would ask both parties to do then, is go back and talk this out between yourselves, to see if there isn't some common ground you can reach that helps both sides. We shouldn't be here today. It isn't right. You can't settle this in court.

"I expect to see all of you back here in a week. What I would like to hear at that time is that you've resolved your differences. If you have not, well, then I will hear the case and make a ruling. But I don't want to have to do that. I really don't.

"This should *not* be argued in a court. You can resolve this on your own. I know you can, if you're willing to try."

The judge then pounded his gavel and walked out of the silent, stunned courtroom. I wasn't sure what had happened, but I knew it wasn't what anyone had expected.

"So what did he say?" Elaine whispered to Rob after the judge had left the courtroom.

Rob shrugged, a kind of hopeless look on his face. "He told us to go back and figure this out for ourselves."

"And if we can't?" Elaine asked.

"Then I guess he'll hear the case although it's clear that he doesn't want to," Rob said.

We all looked at each other. We all had the exact, same question on our minds. Now what? Somehow, I had a feeling that the question would be answered for us, and that events would proceed whether we had anything to say about it or not. I was right.

24

We were mobbed by reporters as we walked out of the courtroom. There were probably three reporters for every member of "the gang of seven." And they all had the same question.

"Do you have any reaction to what the governor just said about you?" the reporter asked me. I could hear the same question asked of the others as we tried to walk down the steps of the courthouse.

I looked over at Elaine and Rob. They clearly had no idea what these reporters were talking about either. "The governor of what?" I asked the reporter.

The reporter almost dropped his microphone. "The Governor of Virginia, Thomas Hilton. He's planning to run for President. He's been campaigning around the country for months."

"Oh, that governor," I said meekly. "He said something about *us?*"

"He made a comment about your club at a press conference this morning," the reporter said, glancing down at his notes. "He said he would do everything in his power to make sure the other students at Roosevelt weren't harassed by Christians trying to impose their narrow views on the other students."

"He said *that?*" I asked, dumbfounded. "Why would the Governor of Virginia care about our Bible Club?"

The reporter just glared back at me. "You're serious?"

"Of course I'm serious," I said defensively. "Why would he care about our club?"

"Because you guys are news, that's why," the reporter said. "And Hilton can take advantage of it. He probably figures that attacking your club will help him run for President.

"Oh, I see," I answered.

"So do you have any comment?" the reporter then asked, thrusting the microphone back in my face.

"Well, um, no, I guess not," I said as the red light glowed on the camera. "I don't know why the governor would attack me. We just want to have a Bible Club. That's all. It's no big deal."

"It is now," the reporter said.

I just moped around the house all morning long on Saturday. At some point, Mom took the phone off the hook for a half hour or so, just to give the family some peace.

It had been complete, utter chaos at our house. The telephone hadn't stopped ringing since the newspaper had screamed the headline at us when we woke up: "Governor Rips into Christian Students."

I felt like a fool, a little piece of a big puzzle I couldn't understand at all. And I felt totally helpless to do anything about it.

Mom said it was all politics, that Governor Thomas Hilton had seen an opportunity to get on television and help himself as he ran for President by attacking us. *We* didn't really matter all that much. We were pawns.

She said Hilton was attacking us because it got him on television and into the news. We were news, and attacking us got him free publicity. It was as simple as that.

I didn't think it was right for him to do that. Mom said that was the way politicians worked. Or, at least, the way *some* politicians worked. They attack and destroy, without worrying too much about the people they are going after.

When I finally got around to calling Elaine late in

the morning, she sounded ecstatic. She loved this stuff, this kind of a fight.

"And the senator called me!" she almost yelled over the phone.

"Senator?" I asked.

"Of Virginia. Senator Johnson Ellicott," she said.

"He called you? Why?"

"To tell me that he supported me, and not to be intimidated by Governor Hilton."

"You're kidding. Why would he do that?"

"Cally, are you serious? You really don't know?"

"Nope. Sorry."

"Well, my folks say it's because Governor Hilton is from one party, and Senator Ellicott is from the other one."

"So they're taking different sides?"

"Yeah, something like that."

Somehow, I had the sneaking suspicion that we would see Senator Ellicott's comments on our little Bible Club on the news tonight, and I told Elaine that. *He* could get on television too, for supporting us.

"Sure, probably," she said. "People are really getting into this," Elaine said, her voice crackling with enthusiasm.

I took a deep breath. "Elaine?"

"Yeah?"

"Isn't all of this getting out of hand? Shouldn't we do something to stop it, maybe drop the Bible Club?"

"Cally!" she exclaimed. "Don't say that. We have to see this through to the end, even if it goes all the way to the Supreme Court and the President of the United States."

"But what will we get out of it? We'll never be able to hold our Bible Club at the rate we're going. People are just going crazy over all of this."

"Oh, I'm not sure our Bible Club matters anymore," Elaine said.

"It doesn't?"

"No, it's the principle of the thing. It's bigger now."

"But I thought all we wanted to do was have a little Bible Club."

"Well, we *did,*" Elaine said evasively. "But now, well, now it's changed, it's bigger, more important."

"Elaine," I said quietly, "I don't think it's right, getting caught up in all these wars between governors and senators and judges and stuff. I just wanted to have a Bible Club."

"Well, it's too late for that now, Cally," Elaine said forcefully. "We have to keep going. We just have to."

"I don't know, Elaine," I answered. "Somehow, it seems like there has to be a better way. There just has to."

"Good luck trying to find it, Cally," Elaine said. "I'm going to keep going. I hope you do too."

----26

So Elaine and I took different paths.

TV cameras and reporters showed up at her house all weekend long. The stream was endless. I had no idea there were so many people who cared about stuff like this.

She was going to be on the "Phil Donahue Show" on Monday. The producer talked to her by phone for an hour on Saturday, and it was all set. She was going to a studio somewhere in Washington, D.C., and they would beam her up by satellite.

On Tuesday Elaine was going to be on "The Today Show" and "Good Morning America." She'd go downtown to a studio somewhere and sit in a chair and talk to the people who hosted those shows from New York.

She also talked to reporters from *People* magazine, *Time, Newsweek*, and several other national magazines and newspapers.

Elaine said it was non-stop. They just kept coming to her house in droves. They were waiting in line to see her. Her mom served coffee to them while they waited in the living room.

They were mostly polite, she said. They mostly asked the same questions. Why are you doing this? What about separation of church and state? Should you talk about God in public schools? What about

Governor Hilton's comments?

Elaine said it was really this last one, the question about Governor Hilton, that had sent the whole thing into outer orbit. Because Hilton was running for President, his comments made the whole thing a *really* big deal. Otherwise, it was interesting, but not a really big deal.

I asked her during my one conversation with her on Sunday night—it was the only time I was able to get through to her on the telephone—if she didn't feel like she'd been used by Hilton.

"Oh, no," Elaine had said breathlessly. "I don't think so. I see this as an opportunity to get the word out about Jesus Christ."

"You do?"

"Sure. I can talk about my faith to every one of these people, and it will reach millions of people."

"But will any of these people put that in their stories?"

"I don't know," Elaine said. "But when I'm doing the TV junk, I can talk about it."

"And will people believe you, do you think?"

"Sure, why not?" Elaine had answered confidently.

I guess that's where I didn't agree with Elaine. I thought it all made her look kind of silly. I didn't think anyone would believe a thirteen-year-old girl talking about her faith in Jesus Christ on national television.

She was right, in one way. It was an opportunity. But, somehow, I didn't think she'd get much of a chance to say more than the guys who win the Super Bowl and blurt into the camera that they want to thank the Lord, or the pitcher who wins the last game of the World Series and says the same thing.

I just didn't think anyone would think more than one second about it. They'd hear it—oh, yeah, she believes in God—and then they'd go onto something else.

Meanwhile, I stopped taking any telephone calls. After I wouldn't talk to the first few reporters who called or showed up, it was like there was some big bulletin board in the sky announcing to everyone that I wasn't talking. The calls and visits just stopped.

Which was just fine and dandy with me. I'd absolutely had enough. I didn't want to talk to another reporter as long as I lived. I had no desire to be "famous." No desire whatsoever.

I had another plan. Or at least the beginning of one. First thing Monday morning, I was going to visit someone else, someone the reporters had told me also wasn't talking to them. I would start there.

There were no police guarding the door to Room 122 when I stopped by after school Monday. There was no gang of cameras and reporters, no crowd of students looking on.

Mrs. Sanders was sitting at her desk, grading papers, when I walked in. She didn't look up, because I didn't say anything right away. She looked awfully tired.

I finally coughed, and she flinched. "Oh, I didn't hear you come in, Cally," she said softly. "Please. Have a seat."

"Thanks," I said, and slid into a seat in the front row.

Mrs. Sanders finished grading the paper she'd been looking at and then moved the pile of papers off to one side of her desk. "So, what can I do for you?" she asked.

"Um, well, I just wanted to talk to you," I stammered, not sure how to begin this conversation.

"How was your weekend? Busy, I'll bet," she said with a smile.

"Yeah, there were lots of reporters who tried to call me. But I stopped talking to them. It's Elaine who's dying to talk to all those people. She thinks it's a good way to get the word out about believing in God."

Mrs. Sanders nodded. "Yes, I can see how Elaine

would feel that way."

"Do *you* think that's the right thing to do?"

Mrs. Sanders looked away. "Oh, I don't know. I suppose it has some usefulness. I guess it reminds people, even briefly, that there's more to life than soap operas, chocolate donuts, McDonald's hamburgers, and Monday night football."

"So you think it's worthwhile, what Elaine is doing?"

"Sure," she said, looking back at me. "Elaine has a noble purpose. She means well."

I just shook my head. "I don't think it does anything. I think it's all crazy, that it makes people crazy. We'll never have our Bible Club, not now. There's no way."

"Yes, I think you're right about that, Cally," Mrs. Sanders said somewhat wistfully.

"Which was supposed to be the whole point of all of this, I thought."

"Yes, it was supposed to be."

"But now Elaine just says that the Bible Club doesn't really matter, that it's all gotten a lot bigger than that."

"Well, in a way, she's right. When Governor Hilton said what he said, this all became a big deal."

"Why did he do that?" I asked, mostly because I didn't know why someone would do such a thing.

"Oh, actually, it's simple," Mrs. Sanders smiled. "If he attacks you, he gets lots of free publicity. He gets on television. It helps him as he tries to run for President. And he picks up the votes of people who might be angry about what you kids are doing."

"So it was a way to get votes?"

"Exactly. It's that simple."

"That's really rotten."

Mrs. Sanders laughed. "Yes, but it's politics."

"Can I ask you something else?"

"Sure," she nodded.

"What's going to happen to you now?"

She looked like she'd been expecting the question because she sighed and clasped her hands on the desk. "That's what I've thought about all weekend long, Cally. That very question."

"You have?"

"Yes, I have, because Kamber told me I wouldn't be rehired next year. He told me to look for another teaching job."

"You mean he fired you?"

Mrs. Sanders shook her head. "No, he didn't fire me, really. He just told me I would not be hired next year, that my contract wouldn't be renewed. It's not the same thing."

"Oh, I see. So what will you do?"

"I haven't decided yet. Probably go to a private school."

"Do you want to stay at Roosevelt?"

Mrs. Sanders looked at me. "You know, actually, I do. I like it here. I think I'm making a difference. I would like to stay here. But Kamber hasn't given me that choice."

"What if I can help? Would you stay?"

Mrs. Sanders smiled. "Cally, that would be nice of you, but I think you'd be wasting your time. I don't think anyone's going to change Kamber's mind."

"Can I at least try?"

"Be my guest. It never hurts to try."

28

I watched "The Today Show" and "Good Morning America" before Mom drove me to school Tuesday morning. The entire school was buzzing about it during homeroom. I ignored all that and moved into Phase Two of my secret plan.

I figured that Kamber would never see me if I tried to make an appointment with him. So, I skipped first period and hung around outside his office until he came out. Then I bolted inside, where his secretaries were, and just went right up to him.

"Mr. Kamber, can I talk to you for a second?"

"Aren't you supposed to be in class, Mr. James?"

"Well, yeah, but I wanted to talk to you. Can I?"

Kamber stared back at me grim-faced. "I'm not sure there's much to talk about—"

"I wanted to talk about Mrs. Sanders, how you fired her," I said quickly.

Kamber's eyes were hot coals of anger. "I didn't fire her. She brought this on herself."

I glanced over at his private office. "Can we just talk about it for a second? Please?"

Kamber sighed. "All right. If you must. But only for a minute or so. I have a full day."

I moved toward his office before he could change his mind. "I promise. Only a minute."

Kamber sat down. "So. I suppose you're all ready for

⓵⓵⑨

arguments in our famous case later this week?"

I looked hard at him. "Mr. Kamber, didn't the judge tell us we were supposed to work this out between ourselves? Didn't he say that?"

Kamber snorted. "He said we were supposed to *try* to work things out. There's a big difference between trying and actually doing so."

"Well, shouldn't we try then?" I persisted.

"OK, fine. I'll listen to anything you have to say." He leaned back in his chair and folded his arms.

"Well, first, I just want to say something about Mrs. Sanders. She really likes Roosevelt. She wants to stay. She doesn't want to go to a private school."

"It's a little too late for that, I'm afraid."

"But why? Why is it too late?"

"Because she chose sides. She made her decision."

"But Mr. Kamber, she didn't choose sides," I said. "All she did was agree to let some students hold a club in her classroom. That's all she did. She didn't say rotten things about you or the school. She didn't hold any press conferences. She didn't go to court."

"But she broke the rules," Kamber insisted. "She disobeyed *me.*"

"Well, she's probably sorry," I sighed. "I'm sure she wishes she'd gotten your permission first."

"But she didn't, did she? And now it's too late."

I leaned forward in my chair. "Mr. Kamber, you shouldn't punish her because of what she believes."

"I'm not punishing her for what she believes," Kamber protested indignantly.

"Yes, you are. She made a mistake. She should have asked you if we could use her room. I know she's sorry about that. But now you're firing her because of what she believes. You think she's on the 'other' side. And that's not right."

"I'm not firing her," Kamber said lamely.

"You're not letting her come back next year. It's just about the same thing."

Kamber glared at me for several long moments. "She can't possibly want to remain here, at Roosevelt, after all that's happened."

"But Mr. Kamber, she does. She wants to teach at Roosevelt. Really she does. She likes it here, just like I do. I want to stay here too. All my friends are here. I hope I don't have to leave."

Our eyes locked for what seemed like an eternity. We were supposed to be mortal enemies. That's the way the newspapers had it, the way the whole world seemed to think about it. He was the big, bad principal who wouldn't let me and a few of the other kids hold a Bible Club at his school.

But, really, we were just two people, caught in something neither of us had planned or dreamed of. I don't even know whether Kamber believed in God or not. I don't think it mattered. I figured he'd get around to figuring out his own life in his own time.

All that mattered right now was whether we could reach across the horrible gap that had opened between the two of us. Was there a bridge there?

"I'll tell you what," Kamber said softly. "If Mrs. Sanders comes and talks to me, maybe we can work something out, just between the two of us."

"Great! That's just great, Mr. Kamber!"

Kamber's face darkened again. "But that doesn't solve our other little problem, you know."

"Just let me worry about that, Mr. Kamber. I have an idea there too. But it'll take some work."

"You don't have a whole lot of time, Cally."

"I know. That's why I have to work fast."

Now came the hard part. I knew that Elaine would be hardest to convince, so I went to the others first.

Before I did that, though, I went back to Mrs. Sanders. I pulled her from the classroom at the start of second period and told her what Kamber had told me. She was dumbfounded.

"You *didn't!*" she exclaimed.

"I did," I beamed. "And he said to come talk to him. No cameras, no reporters, no PTA members, no lawyers. I think you guys can work something out."

Mrs. Sanders just shook her head. "I can't believe it's that simple."

"Just go talk to him, Mrs. Sanders," I said. "I think Kamber's probably an OK guy. I think it'll work out."

Then I spent the rest of the day cornering each member of "the gang of seven" between classes, except Elaine, and tried my idea out on them. As I'd hoped, they were all willing to give it a try.

Sheryl grumbled, which I'd expected. But I think she was a little jealous that Elaine had become so famous in all of this, and she was definitely willing to try anything that might end it all.

Jason was convinced it wouldn't work, that Kamber wouldn't go for it and that it was a little wacky. But he was willing to try.

Barry was quite sure that someone else would come

up with some reason why my plan wouldn't work. But he too was at least willing to try it out on Kamber and everyone else now involved.

And then there was Elaine. She wanted to fight this thing to the death if she had to. She wanted to go to the Supreme Court, where she would undoubtedly hold a monster press conference with hundreds of reporters hanging on her every word.

Someday, Elaine could do just that, with some other cause. Right now, all I wanted to do was stop all the fighting. In a way, it reminded me of what I spent half my life doing at home since Dad had vanished.

Because I was the oldest, it seemed like I was always stopping fights and shouting matches around the house. Chris would be pounding on Karen for some reason, and I'd wade in and calm both of them down. Or Susan would be crying because Jana had said something mean to her, and I'd sit them both down and find out what had happened.

This was no different, really. I was just trying to stop a fight that had gotten slightly out of control.

To be honest, it was Mom who'd given me the idea. We'd been talking about things late one night, and she'd just sort of mentioned something to me in passing. We'd talked about it some more and, before I knew what had happened, her little idea had suddenly become *my* idea.

I remember seeing the funniest smile on her face as she watched me get excited about the idea and the possibility that maybe I could get everyone to stop fighting over the Bible Club.

"Cally, I think you really have something there," Mom had said to me. "I think it just might work."

"Yeah, I think so too," I'd said. My mind had been racing at the time, as I thought about how I'd go about getting everyone to agree.

"You know that Elaine will be the hardest to convince," she'd said. "She's all set to fight this thing."

"I know," I'd said grimly.

"What you might want to do," she'd suggested gently, "is invite her out, maybe go to McDonald's after school, just the two of you, and talk to her about it there."

I'd nearly fallen over backward. "Take Elaine out? Like on a date?"

"No, not on a date," Mom had smiled. "Just take her to McDonald's, buy her a milkshake and some french fries. Believe me, you'll have an easier time of it."

"I don't know," I'd said, shaking my head. "That sounds like a weird way of going about things."

"Trust me on this, Cally. OK?" Mom had said.

So I asked Elaine to stop off at McDonald's with me after school.

"But what about tennis practice?" she'd asked me suspiciously.

"I, um, you know, don't really have to go today," I'd said evasively. "They're working on doubles today, and I don't need to practice that."

Elaine had clearly not been convinced. "So why do you want to go to McDonald's? And how will we get home after that?"

"I'll walk you back to your house. It's only six or seven blocks."

"But back to your house?"

"I'll run home. I need the exercise anyway. So will you go or not?"

Elaine had sighed. "Oh, all right. I guess we should talk about our strategy for the hearing. We can talk about it there."

"Yeah, that's right. "We can talk about it there."

----30

It wasn't a date, really. Not an actual date, where you ask someone out, like to the movies, and then you talk about mushy stuff afterward. I just wanted to talk to Elaine, and Mom had said this was the way to go about it. OK, so I bought Elaine's milkshake and fries with my own money. And it was just the two of us. It wasn't a date. It just wasn't.

My plan, the one I'd come up with after Mom had "suggested" it to me, was actually pretty simple.

Down in Alabama, before we moved to Washington, there had been a run-down trailer parked on the street next to our elementary school. We used to go out to that old trailer for special classes during the day. Sometimes we'd have special art classes in it or maybe a music class. There had also been these two old ladies who'd read to us from the Bible. I'd never thought much about it until now. How had they been able to do that? I wondered after Mom had mentioned it.

They'd been able to do that, we finally concluded, because the trailer was parked on the street. It wasn't actually on the school's property. It was very close by, but it wasn't actually on the school grounds.

Maybe we could do the same thing here.

As I slid into my seat, in the booth at the back of the restaurant, I handed Elaine her fries and milkshake.

She smiled at me. "Thanks, Cally. This is nice. I'm glad you invited me."

"Well, yeah, me too," I mumbled. I could feel my face starting to get red so I changed the subject. Fast. "You know, I saw you on those shows. You were great. You didn't look nervous or anything."

"Boy, I felt nervous," she admitted. "I was so nervous, I couldn't sit still. My mouth was so dry I wasn't sure I'd be able to talk right."

"Well, it didn't look that way," I assured her. "You looked like you'd done that sort of thing all your life."

"You know, this has been kind of fun, all this stuff about the Bible Club," she said. "I've gotten used to the reporters by now. They don't bother me as much as they did."

"Yeah, I guess you can get used to anything after a while."

"I mean, it's actually sort of neat, now," she continued, almost as if she were talking to herself and not me. "I almost know what the reporters are going to ask me. They always ask the same questions."

I looked down at the table. I figured it was now or never. If I didn't talk to Elaine soon about my plan, I never would.

"Hey!" I said a little too loudly. "Don't you think we oughtta try to get our Bible Club back, a real club? If we can, I mean?"

Elaine shook her head grimly. "I don't know, Cally. My folks say it's too late for that. I think they're probably right. It's too late. We'll just have to fight it out."

"But then we'll never actually have a club," I said, gazing intently at the tabletop.

"I know," Elaine agreed. "And that's too bad. It really is."

I looked up quickly. "What if we could still have it?

What if we could actually do something and end all of this? Would you go for that?"

"Sure, but . . ." Elaine stopped talking and began to stare at me. "Cally, what have you been up to?"

I tried not to smile. But I'm sure it sort of leaked out both sides of my mouth. "Oh, I've just been talking. To Mrs. Sanders. To Kamber. Mrs. Sanders is gonna keep her job at Roosevelt, I think."

"That's great," Elaine said suspiciously.

I took a deep breath. "And I've also talked to the others."

"The others?"

"You know, from our Bible study group. Barry and Sheryl and Jason."

"About what?"

"About my plan," I said quietly.

"Your plan?"

"To actually have a Bible Club. I think I have a plan that could stop all the fighting."

Elaine's eyes narrowed. "And how will you do that?"

I seized the opening with everything I had. "It's simple. I think we can get Kamber to agree to it. They could probably use the trailer for other stuff, not just our Bible Club. I'm sure they can think of all sorts of uses for it—"

"Cally!" Elaine said sharply. "What are you talking about?"

"A trailer," I said sheepishly. "I'm talking about a trailer. They could park it on the street, right next to the school. It wouldn't be on the school grounds, but we could hold our Bible Club in it. We did something like that at my school in Alabama. I'd forgotten about it until Mom reminded me."

Elaine nodded. "I should have known. So this is

your mom's idea?"

"Well, sort of. It's mine. But it's hers too."

"So Kamber gets this trailer and parks it on the street, and we hold our club in it. It's not on school property, so Roosevelt won't care. Is that it?"

"Yeah, that's it."

"It's a *dumb* idea," Elaine said bitterly.

I tried not to flinch. I was half-expecting that she'd react this way. It's not easy to stop being famous. "Why?" I asked quietly.

"Because," she said flatly, "it won't work. The trailer would be on city property, and then they'd object. And we'd still have a big fight."

"I don't think so," I countered. "I think it would all work out. You'll see."

"No, it won't," she said. "Kamber will never go for it."

"I think he will," I said, staring straight at her. "But only if you're willing to try it. Will you, Elaine?"

"I can't believe you don't want to keep fighting. I can't believe you'd just give up like this."

"I'm not giving up. I just want to stop fighting. And I want to have the Bible Club. That's all."

Elaine and I looked at each other. The restaurant was almost silent, except for a squeal from a two- or three-year-old on the other side of the place. Right then, at that very moment, there were only two people in the whole world.

And then I could see that everything would be all right. The look in Elaine's eyes changed. Gone were all the national TV shows. Just like that. I could see Elaine saying good-bye to all the national attention. I knew it wasn't easy.

"All right," she sighed. "I'll give it a try. Let's go talk to Kamber and see if your plan will work."

──31

Roosevelt's auditorium was absolutely packed.
There were zillions of reporters everywhere. I'd never
seen so much electronic equipment. I counted at least
thirty different cameras.

How do all these people hear about things? I wondered as I stood by myself offstage, behind the thick
curtains that hid the backstage area from the auditorium seats.

Elaine and I had talked to Kamber Thursday morning, the day before we were all supposed to go back
to court and argue before the judge. We'd talked, and
then we'd all decided to hold a press conference.
Together.

The trucks and camera crews and the reporters and
all the other assorted media types, with their boom
microphones and long cables and recorders, started to
show up just after lunchtime. By 2 P.M. Thursday the
whole school was buzzing. Nobody got any work
done.

Someone nudged my shoulder. I turned to see Rob
standing over me. "You ready for this?" he asked.

"Sure. Why not?" I shrugged.

"You know, I've been meaning to tell you. This is
quite a plan you've come up with."

"Thanks," I mumbled.

Rob smiled. "When Jesus gave His Sermon on the

Mount, one of the things He talked about was being a peacemaker."

"I think I remember that," I said. "Blessed are the peacemakers . . ."

"For they shall be called the sons of God," Rob said, finishing the verse for me.

"Yeah, something like that. Only I don't know if I'm a son of God."

"Yes, you are," Rob said softly. "In the truest sense of the word. I just wanted to tell you that I'm proud of you. It takes real courage to do what you've done, with so much attention being paid to this."

We both looked up then, as Kamber and Elaine strode purposefully onto the stage from the other direction. I was thankful to get out of our conversation. Rob and I both watched as Kamber leaned forward to speak into all of the microphones jammed onto the podium.

"We have an announcement to make, Elaine Cimons and I," Kamber said. The TV cameras whirred. The reporters scribbled onto their notebooks. They were ready for more fireworks.

"We, Roosevelt, have decided to settle this dispute. We've decided to rent a trailer and place it on one of the side streets, next to the school. Elaine's Bible Club will then be allowed to meet there regularly."

"Is that OK with you, Elaine?" one of the reporters shouted out. "Is that what you want?"

Elaine glanced over at me. I knew it wasn't what she wanted. What Elaine *really* wanted was for the whole thing to go on, so the cameras would keep coming back. But she would not waver. Not now. I knew she wouldn't.

"It's what's best for everybody," she said to the mob. "It's what the Bible Club wants. It's the best